DIVINE AWAKENING

THE DIVINITIES
BOOK FOUR

LIA DAVIS

Divine Awakening

The Divinities, book 4

© copyright 2016 Lia Davis

Published by Davis Raynes Publishing Group, LLC

PO Box 224 | Middleburg, Fl. 32050

Cover by and Formatting by Glowing Moon Designs

www.AuthorLiaDavis.com

DIVINE AWAKENING

A mother's love is her greatest power.

Divinity witch, Desiree Sanders has made a lot of bad choices in her life, but trusting the demoness, Samoan should earn her the award for traitor of the millennium. After several failed attempts to set things right, Desiree turns to the dark, sexy Death Demon, Lex for help saving her son and ending the war.

There's no darker place than the soul of a demon.

Divinity guardian, Alexander, AKA Lex, has hardened his heart and locked away emotions following the betrayal of his mate over three hundred years ago. Until he meets the quiet and beautiful Desiree, and the walls around his heart start to crumble. When she calls him for help, broken and scared, he can't deny her, and the urge to claim her for his own becomes an overwhelming need.

Trapped in the Underworld as the war between witches and demons escalates, Lex and Desiree must face their pasts and their fears—and open their hearts—if they are to find a way out. Meanwhile, the Divinities in the natural world prepare for a battle that is no longer just dark versus light. If lost, it could mean the end of life as they know it.

CHAPTER ONE

"They're here," Lex said with a growl as he, Desiree, Zach, and Lydia crept along the dark corridors of Khan's castle. The smell of sulfur and dirt tingled his nose. Even though Lex had a home in the Underworld, he didn't spend much time there. Not since Khan had taken over, anyway. "The hounds are separated and masked with a spell."

His keen sense of dark magic came from his Death Demon half and his connection to Hecate— Goddess of Witchcraft. Khan may believe he'd hidden Teddy-Bear, but not from everyone. *The fool bastard.*

Lex fisted his hands. It took every fiber of his being to hold onto his control. The hounds couldn't survive spit apart for much longer. As Siamese twins, their magic and souls were linked. They were growing weaker by the moment.

Reaching out to mind link with the hounds, he found Teddy first in a room a few feet away. Then he heard the faint *thump, thump* of the hellhound's heartbeat.

"He's alive. Thank the goddess." *We're coming, buddy.*

A low growl from Lydia at his back told him she wasn't pleased with the hounds being apart. "Do you know where they are?"

With a short nod, he advanced down a hallway in quick strides. He uncurled his magic, letting it flow wildly within and waited for an attack. Lydia, Zach, and Desiree followed, having to fall into a light jog to keep up with him.

"Things are too quiet." Zach spoke in a hushed tone; concern and fear of what was ahead of them drifted from him. Dark, elfin magic rose within the male and reached out to Lex's senses.

Yeah, things were too quiet.

Stopping a few feet down the hall, Lex stopped and faced them. He flicked a hard stare to the door they had stopped a few feet from. Cold, lethal power rose in his veins. The hounds were his family—what little he had left—and he'd be damned if Khan got away with harming them. "Teddy is in there. Zach and Lydia, you get him. Desiree and I will get Bear. We'll meet at the Divinity House."

The reason for not busting down the door and freeing Teddy was that Bear's heartbeat sounded stronger. Teddy would need Lydia's healing touch. Lex figured it'd be quicker to rush down the hall and collect Bear while Lydia healed Teddy.

When they reached the door, Lex didn't bother to check the lock. He just plowed through the thick wood, tearing the thing off its hinges. The room was empty except for a large cage in the center with Bear standing in it, teeth bared.

The hound met Lex's gaze and snarled, "The place is going to blow."

"How long?" Lex snapped the lock on the cage with quick efficiency, not surprised that Khan had set the trap. One reason it was so quiet and they were able to get in without *Regal* guards coming down on them. *Should have known.*

"Not sure. Maybe two minutes or less."

Fear gripped his heart and squeezed. They had to get out of there. He wouldn't lose Desiree when he'd just found her.

Desiree moved to the opening and stuck her head

out. Lex moved closer to her, too aware of her whirlwind of emotions: Anger, fear, and a desperate need to find her son. "Bear, go find your brother and get out of here."

"What are you doing? There's no time." The hound paused once they'd exited into the hall.

"We'll get out. Get Teddy, Zach, and Lydia out," Lex barked, then grabbed Desiree's hand and tugged her down the hall in the opposite direction that he'd sent Bear. A growl at his back was Bear's final protest before the hound took off to find the others.

Desiree tensed up next to Lex but didn't jerk her hand from his. In fact, she seemed to accept his touch with ease, like it helped soothe her anxiety. *Good.* He needed her touch just as much. Needed to know she was safe.

Her power was close to the surface, nipped at his own. He ignored it. "Can you sense Mathew?"

She trembled at the mention of her son's name and shook her head. "For a moment, I thought I could. But he's not here. At least, not anymore. We need to get out of here."

She didn't need to tell him twice. Focusing on his home, he teleported them. Materializing in his living room, he released Desiree's hand and stalked to the bedroom, needing to put some distance between them. The female made him ache with need. The urge to take her in every way possible was almost overwhelming.

Fuck. He didn't want a mate, yet he'd found one. The pull to Desiree was too strong. He wouldn't be able to keep his hands off her much longer.

Boom! The house shook from the blast of Khan's castle. Closing his eyes, he searched for the connection he had with the hellhounds. Relief flooded him when he felt them, alive. *They made it out.*

Suddenly, a rush of power rippled across his skin, and he whirled around to meet Desiree's stare. Standing in the doorway of his bedroom, wide-eyed she said, "All the portals just opened."

"Hecate," he called out.

She replied back telepathically. *"I felt it, and I'm handling it. You have to find Khan and get the Dark Sinew from him. However, once I close the portals you'll have to find another way to return Earthside."*

Then the goddess was gone, cutting the telepathic connection. He sighed. She'd have to use the power of three plus the Sinew to close all of the portals. As far as he knew, no one but the gods could cross from one realm to another once they were locked. But Hecate had said to find another way out.

He had no idea how to do that.

Returning his attention to Desiree, he said, "Hecate will be closing the portals. We will be stuck here for a while."

Stuck in Hell with a Death Demon without the earth her Divinity half craved... The magic in the Underworld was heavy and dark. She needed to get home.

Folding her arms, she glared at Lex while trying to tamp down the rush of desire his presence caused. "I hope you know of a way to get back home."

He grunted and pushed past her as if ending the conversation.

Oh no, he doesn't. She whirled around and followed him through the living room to the study across from his bedroom. "There is another way out, right?"

Another grunt was her answer.

She pursed her lips and studied him as he pulled

several books from the shelves. "What are you looking for?"

"A way out."

Well, didn't that answer her questions? She rolled her eyes and left the room. Fine. If he weren't going to talk to her, she'd search for her own way home. Pushing out the back door, she scowled at the gloom of the Underworld. The air held hints of rosemary and sulfur. Reminded her of Samoan's scent, only not as sweet.

Breathing deeply, she closed her eyes and called her *Porter* half to the surface, beseeching the lost souls she felt in every shadow of the Underworld to aid her in crossing to the natural realm. Instead of helping her, they attacked. Rushed around her, through her, raging like angry beams of light.

What the fuck? There were too many of them tearing at her. They called her a witch and thought she was responsible for trapping them there. Many even screamed in her mind. She curled into a ball on the ground, her arms wrapped protectively around her head.

Pain rocketed through her, and she screamed out as she blasted the spirits with everything she had stored up and hadn't gotten to use at the castle. Instantly, they vanished.

Uncurling and pushing to her feet, she met the green eyes of a hellhound. He watched her with eyes much too humanlike. Then a shudder went through its body as it...shifted?

A moment later, Mathew stood in front of her. *My son.* Her heart lurched in her chest and tears filled her eyes. "Matty," she breathed, making the kid narrow his eyes in curiosity.

"No one calls me that. Who are you?"

Chest tightening, she knew he wouldn't remember her. Yet, she had to try. Tears filled her eyes. "I'm your mother."

When she stepped forward, he backed up, shaking his head. "My mother's dead."

Anger rose up then. Samoan would die when Desiree found the bitch. "Samoan lied to you like she lied to me."

Just then, darkness settled around them, making the gloomy realm almost lightless. The air grew heavier with black magic. It was as if something had changed the Underworld.

Matty looked at the sky and scowled. "It has begun." Then he took off into the forest.

She charged after him but stopped short when Lex materialized in front of her. "We have bigger issues. This,"—he pointed to the black clouds swirling in the sky—"isn't part of locking down the portals. Too much energy is building, and possibly leaking into the other realms."

"What?" She stared at him.

"You said Khan was making a dark version of the Sinew."

She nodded and then froze. *Fuck.* "He succeeded."

"It seems so." Lex scrubbed a hand through his long, black hair. "Hecate said we have to find it."

It was her turn to scowl. "Our best bet for finding Khan just got away."

CHAPTER TWO

*L*ex watched Desiree storm back into the house and slam the door behind her. Why hadn't she felt the curse moving in before she tried to jump realms? Working his jaw, he advanced toward the manor.

Confirmation that she hadn't told him everything about her abilities settled in the front of his thoughts.

The moment he entered the house, a sinking feeling tightened his gut. It was too quiet. He moved his feet faster and came up short when he entered the living room. Desiree stumbled to the sofa and sat while holding her head. Heart falling to his feet, he rushed forward. Her skin was cool to the touch, but her pulse was steady even though she was low on energy. Most likely from fending off the revenant attack. He gathered her up in his arms and sat back on the couch.

After removing her shoes and quickly inspecting her for external injuries, he cradled her. "Rest."

The lost souls had sucked the energy from her, most likely trying to use her as their gateway instead of working with her. It was the curse of the dark power.

She nodded but didn't relax. Caressing her cheek with his fingertips, he sighed and allowed himself to feel compassion—something he hadn't done since his first mate had betrayed him and his village.

From the moment he and Desiree briefly locked gazes at the Oceanway Coven after the attack, he'd known she was his to claim. He'd also smelled Samoan on her, which had made him push her away, not able to trust anyone working with the enemy.

When Desiree had called him for help and had explained that she was being blackmailed, he couldn't deny her. She was his mate. The primal need to be with her, to protect her, overruled logic. However, it didn't excuse the fact that she could have told someone...sought help to bring Samoan down.

"I don't like it here." Her whispered tone broke through his thoughts.

Placing a kiss on her forehead, he inhaled her floral scent. His mate. So beautiful and complicated. "I don't like being trapped."

His admission made her lift her head and gaze into his eyes. "I don't like the dark. I sleep with some kind of light on."

He smiled. She was more powerful than she believed and didn't like the dark. "Tell me something else about you."

One corner of her sensual lips dipped in a half frown, and she crinkled her nose. "Like what?"

"What's your favorite color, foods, your passions in life?"

Again she frowned. "My favorite color is red, and I love pasta." She cocked her head to the side as she studied him. A slow smiled formed. "I love life and helping others. And you are distracting me."

"Is it working?"

"Maybe. What about you? What's your passion?"

His body tensed. Really, he should have known his attempt to get her to relax would backfire on him. "Protecting my family."

There was too much of an edge to his tone, and Desiree picked up on it. He saw it in her eyes. Twisting so she could straddle his lap, she cupped his face in her hands. Out of reflex, he gripped her hips. His cock filled and hardened.

She stared into his gaze for several moments before she spoke. "Tell me what happened. Who hurt your heart?"

"It was a long time ago." To keep her from insisting on an answer, he kissed her.

She froze at first, then returned the kiss, meeting his tongue with hers. A groan escaped him, and he wrapped his arms around her, sinking his fingers into her waist-length hair and fisting the strands.

He tightened his hold on her, meshing their bodies together. Hunger like no other filled him. Desiree's scent intoxicated him, made him crave more than he should. He broke the kiss and nipped at her jaw then trailed his tongue down her neck. A soft groan escaped from her, and her body melted into him. A silent approval.

His fangs—those he'd gotten from being a Death Demon—lowered. The steady *thump, thump* of her heartbeat called to him, but it was her scent that begged him to sink his fangs into her, to taste her.

Claim her.

Fuck. No.

He picked her up, moving her to the couch cushion beside him, and left the room, putting distance between them. *Damnit.* He was not impulsive. And he damn sure wasn't going to take her blood and bind them together. Not yet.

He scowled as he entered the study, aware that she was on his heels. The more they were together, the more he wanted her. If Jagger were there, the male would tease Lex and point out that he had feelings for the beautiful strawberry-blond.

Lex's chest tightened. Jagger wasn't there, and couldn't come to him. No one outside the Underworld could help. A growl rumbled from his chest. There was only one person who could possibly help them now.

He so didn't want to go there. Yet, he didn't have a choice. Khan needed to be stopped. Especially since he now had a Dark Sinew with unpredictable powers.

"What's wrong?" Desiree's tone was soft, but he saw the disappointment in her eyes.

"We need to find Kahn and get the Dark Sinew before he uses it in whatever evil plot he has going." Avoidance was good, right? He wasn't ready to let Desiree know how much she affected him. Although, she may already know. He cursed again and gave her his back.

A few moments of silence passed, then he heard

her footsteps fade off to the living room. He released a sigh.

Just then, a knock sounded on his door. Every hair stood at attention, and every muscle tensed. He didn't have friends on this side. And no one would dare disturb him.

He flashed to the door and yanked the thing open. Ryn, the *Lackey* demon who'd helped Kristof and Angelica escape Demetrius's cells stood on the other side. Only the demon wasn't a *Lackey* anymore. Apparently, Hecate had upgraded his power. Plus, the male had bulked up in the few weeks since Samoan had used him as a whipping boy and tortured him for information.

Ryn held up his right arm, exposing Hecate's wheel etched on the inside of his wrist. "I've been branded." He frowned and glanced behind him as if sensing something. "Hecate sent me to this realm before she went to find Zach and Lydia. I wasn't sure why until everything went on lockdown and I felt your presences."

Uncertainty rolled off the male in waves. Lex stepped aside and said, "Come in."

When Ryn stepped into the house, Lex closed the door behind him and led the demon to the study. "We need to find a way out. Hecate said to find the

Dark Sinew. I'm not sure why or how, so I need to visit Xara."

"You're joking, right?" Lex raised a brow at the male's outburst. Ryn paled before answering his own question. "I guess not."

"I need her help to find Khan, and I need to see what she knows about the Dark Sinew." Lex studied Ryn for several long moments. "But I have to go alone. That means you must stay here with Desiree."

Lex must have growled while voicing the latter because the corner of Ryn's mouth lifted slightly as his crimson eyes flashed a little brighter. "Desiree isn't my type. She doesn't have the right equipment to spark my interests."

Understanding dawned, but Lex still didn't like leaving Desiree. Especially since he didn't know how long he would be gone. The thought of being away from her made him edgy. However, he had no choice. He sure as hell wasn't going to summon the dragon oracle there. No, Lex's home was his, and he didn't need Xara snooping around it, finding things she could use to bargain.

"Look, Hecate kicked my ass in training the last few days. I know it doesn't seem like a long time, and I know I need far more training, but she sent me here to help. She must have some faith in me." Ryn raised his brow, and a wide grin spread across his lips.

The ex-*Lackey* had a point. Although it wasn't Ryn's ability to protect Desiree that concerned Lex. The male had just gotten the power upgrade a few days ago. "How stable is your power?"

"Stable enough."

Lex clenched his jaw and stared at the male, another low growl escaping him. "Now is not the time to get fucking cocky."

Ryn's gaze darkened, making his eyes look black. "My father was a *Regal*, my mother was a *Lackey*. When Khan took over, he tortured my parents, killing them and suppressing my *Regal* power before throwing me in with the rest of his slaves."

If Lex had doubts about Ryn's loyalty, he didn't anymore. "Hecate unlocked them."

Ryn simply nodded. Lex moved to the back window and narrowed his gaze at the line of trees on the edge of his yard. An iridescent rippling blurred one of the trunks. Opening his senses, Lex picked up on Mathew's scent and magical signature. Curious, Lex stepped to the back door and opened it. Mathew didn't leave.

Lex got right to the point. "Samoan lied to you. She stole you from your mother."

After a few moments, Mathew disappeared without a word.

"I've seen that kid around the castle. He doesn't talk to anyone but Samoan."

At Ryn's words, Lex glanced over his shoulder. "Then he's loyal to her. Her spy?"

Ryn shook his head. "I don't think so. It's like he knows he doesn't belong. So I wouldn't worry about him right now. Although, he most likely knows where Khan and Samoan are."

Movement behind Ryn brought Lex's attention to Desiree. He narrowed his eyes at her. Her hair was wet, indicating that she'd taken a quick shower, which explained why she hadn't shown up when Ryn knocked on the door.

She glanced from Lex to Ryn then back again. "Who are you talking about?"

Ignoring her question, Lex crossed the living room to her. "I have to leave for a few days. Ryn will stay with you. I don't expect Khan or Samoan to come here."

When he raised his hand to caress her cheek, she blocked it, hardening her stare. "I'm going with you."

He growled, "No, you're not."

Pursing her lips, she folded her arms. "Yes, I am."

Lex stepped closer to her, his hands fisting at his

sides. When he got within a few inches of her, she pressed the palm of her right hand to his chest. Her *Porter* gifts ran wild inside and around her, calling to his *Porter* side. He'd have to ask her about the power she hid from everyone.

Flicking a gaze to her forearm, he froze, his heart going still for a brief moment at the sight of her Divinity Rose.

Divinities—witches blessed by Hecate to possess god-like powers and strengths—were born with a single red rose with green leaves and a stem. When they found a mate, a second, faded rose appeared beside it. Once the mating bond was complete, the rose brightened to match the one they'd been born with. Desiree had that faded rose. She also had a smaller, dark red rose growing from the base of the stem, representing her son.

He wasn't going to ask when the faded rose had appeared. He already knew it was around the time they'd first met. The same time the mating urge had risen up within him.

"That"—he pointed to the Divinity Roses—"is the reason you stay here."

Narrowing her crystal blue gaze on him, she pushed him, throwing him off balance a little. "Just because the Fates believe we are mates, doesn't mean you have the right to boss me around. I'm going. I'm helping to end this war because I feel responsible."

The last statement was spoken softer, and her voice cracked.

He dipped his head and brushed his lips against hers. What he'd meant to be a quick kiss turned into a passionate, raw need to possess Desiree. She wrapped her arms around him, scoring his shoulders with her nails. A growl rumbled from him, and his body hummed as desire raced through his veins.

He licked the seam of her lips and moaned as she opened and twined her tongue with his. Magic enveloped them, but he couldn't tell if it was his or hers. A combination of both, maybe. Grabbing her ass, he lifted so she could wrap her legs around his waist. When she started to grind against him, he almost lost it and stripped her bare.

The clearing of a throat brought him back to reality. Breaking the kiss, he glared at Ryn and snarled. The demon raised a brow.

Just then, Desiree wiggled out of his arms, sliding her feet to the ground. "I, um..." She sighed and moved a few feet away from Lex. It was all he could do to keep from grabbing her and hauling her to his room. Desiree seemed to recover faster than he when she folded her arms and said, "When are we leaving?"

"If you don't let her go, she'll follow anyway. Even sneak past me," Ryn stated matter-of-factly. "It's better that the three of us go together. I'm sure the residents of the Underworld aren't happy with either of you. Since you are trapped here until you find the Dark Sinew, the buddy system would be best."

Ryn had a point. Lex worked his jaw and locked gazes with Desiree. "We work together, and I need you by my side. It's not a command. It's a request."

She smiled, and her shoulders relaxed. "Deal. Mathew can't be harmed."

Her eyes shone with unshed tears, breaking his heart and bringing back memories. If he could have done something to save his family, he would have. Closing the gap between them, he caressed Desiree's cheek with his knuckles. "I promise. We'll bring Mathew back with us."

"Thank you." She hugged him tightly for a long moment before lifting her gaze back to his. "Let's go see the dragon oracle."

CHAPTER THREE

*N*oah sat in his recliner in the family room of the Daniels house at the Maxville Coven. His family surrounded him, reading over archives to find a way to get Lex and Desiree out of the Underworld. "I'm afraid we just have to hope they will find a way out."

"Lex knows the Underworld. Remember, Ryn is there, too. Between the three of them, they will make it out," Jagger added.

Noah nodded. Right after the portals had been locked down, Hecate briefed them on some rules, so to speak. She'd told them about Ryn and his new *Regal* status thanks to the goddess and his genetics.

"I hate not knowing how to break a curse. I fear the hold on the portals will only last for a short time despite using the Sinew and the power of three to close them." Noah continued to flip through the pages of the old texts and shuffle through the ancient scrolls.

The sound of the doorbell made him raise his head. He caught the equally curious gaze of his wife. Vanessa stood. "I'll get it."

A hint of dark power brushed against Noah's awareness. When he glanced to Zach to motion him to accompany Vanessa, his grandson was already following Ma out of the room.

"Papa, could we ask the Dark Divine to help us search for Khan?" Lydia asked.

Shaking his head slowly, he thought about it while studying his new granddaughter-in-law—well, soon-to-be. She and Zach hadn't gone through with their handfasting yet. Although the two *were* bound by magic and blood, which was stronger than any ceremony Noah could perform. "We would need a lot more power than the covens would be willing to hand over. Even if it meant ending Khan's reign in Hell."

Lydia stiffened and jerked her gaze to the family room entrance. Curious, Noah followed her gaze. A moment later, Zach entered, carrying an unconscious Sindee Donnelly—Dark Divine and lawyer for most of the U.S. covens.

Kalissa gasped and rose to her feet. "What happened?"

When she released a sob, Ayden hugged her and gently steered her from the sofa. By that time, Lydia was in full healer mode. "Lay her on the couch."

Once Zach did as Lydia asked, Vanessa came into the room with a man Noah hadn't met before but had heard a great deal about. Leland Donnelly.

"Leland." Noah addressed the priest of the Charlotte Coven, the man who was also Sindee's brother.

Leland gave a short nod and frowned. "I apologize for my unannounced visit, but I didn't know where else to bring her. The elf in the gatehouse sent us through."

Nodding, Noah faced Sindee, watching Lydia assess her injuries. "Jordon must have recognized Sindee."

Lydia hovered her hands over Sindee, starting at her head and moving down to her booted feet. Lydia removed the other female's footwear. Noah guessed to make her feel more comfortable. Frowning, Lydia glanced up to Leland. "What is her gift?"

"She's telepathic."

Lydia closed her eyes briefly but nodded and

went back to work. Noah moved in closer. "Why does it matter?"

Lydia pulled the coffee table closer to the sofa and sat on it. "Because many telepaths will kind of shut down their minds when badly injured. From what I can tell...umm, she seems drained of her magic."

Leland fisted his hands at his sides. "Khan."

The demon's name was spoken with the venom of a thousand vipers. Noah agreed with Leland's anger. However, channeling the rage wasn't going to help them. "The last we heard, which was a few days ago, Sindee had gone missing. None of us could contact her, and you apparently didn't get my messages."

Leland avoided eye contact and instead focused on his sister as he spoke. "I haven't checked email since she was taken." He paused and took a deep breath, then exhaled. "The demons waited for her to get off work, then took her. I found her about an hour ago at our cabin in the Rockies, drained of all but a small amount of her power. Will she be okay?"

The latter was asked of Lydia, who responded quietly. "I will need your permission to share my and Zach's power with her to wake her. Then it will be up to her to rest and restore her energy."

When Leland didn't answer right away, Lydia stood and walked to him, stopping a half a foot from him. Leland's gaze narrowed, then a bright flash of his magic rippled through his irises. "You're a vampire."

Lydia shrugged. "I'm a Divinity with the healer's touch, who was cursed to be a vamp. Zach is my bonded mate and a dark elf. You did the right thing by bringing her here."

Understanding lit up Leland's features, and he faced Noah. "I didn't believe the rumors that the Divinities were as powerful as they appeared. But I was wrong. Everyone is wrong. You are all even *more* formidable." He turned back to Lydia. "You have my permission to heal my sister. I will be forever in your debt."

Noah clasped a hand on Leland's shoulder. "We may need to collect on it soon." He motioned to the entryway. "Let's give my grandson and his mate some space."

Ayden, Kalissa, Khloe, and Jagger gathered up their tablets and laptops and moved to the library, while Noah led Leland and Vanessa to his basement study that Zach liked to call "Papa's Man Cave."

Once in the study, Noah grabbed two beers from the small fridge. Sitting in his recliner, he handed

Leland one of the longnecks. "We have two of our own trapped in the Underworld."

"Trapped, how?"

Noah sighed. "Right. You haven't checked messages. I understand why. Khan has somehow created a dark version of the Sinew. Our guess is that he used Dark Divine magic to create it. Which would explain what happened to Sindee. He used the dark power to open all the gates to the Underworld. Hecate, Lydia, and Zach locked them down, but we aren't sure how long that will last. A Divinity from the Oceanway Coven and one of the Death Demons Hecate sent to the Divinities as guardians didn't make it out when the portals closed."

Leland glanced from Noah to Vanessa. "I'm so far out of the loop, and not because I don't check my messages as often as I should. I thought I could shield my coven from the war. Sindee's abduction showed me that we're not untouchable."

Vanessa covered Leland's hand. "Many of the Dark Divine are afraid to come out of hiding. Since you have the largest number of Dark Divine in your coven, it's understandable that you want to keep them safe."

"No. I could have asked for volunteers to join the

Divinities in the fight." Leland leaned back on the sofa and took a drink of his beer.

"Stop beating yourself up. You were protecting your coven." Noah studied the other man. Leland didn't have a dark rose, or a Divine Rose on his arm. Although Noah shouldn't be surprised. Not every *magickin* born to a Divinity parent is blessed with a Divine gift or marked by the Divine Rose. "Can I ask you a personal question?"

Leland locked gazes with him. "Sindee is my half-sister. We share the same mother. My father was human." He chuckled and added, "Even though she's five years older, I still protect her like an older brother. And she lets me."

"Sindee has a kind heart."

A smile widened Leland's mouth. "That is true." Then he sat up straight and listened. "She's awake."

"You two are welcome to stay in one of the guest cottages. Just ask Zach to show you which one." Noah stood and followed the other witch up the stairs, Vanessa right behind him.

Before going to the family room, Leland turned and shook Noah's hand. "Anything you need, just ask."

"When Sindee is well enough, I'll need you to ask your Dark Divine to volunteer. My visions are keeping me up at night. Opening the gates to Hell was only the beginning of Khan's plan." Noah frowned, fear burning in his gut.

Leland nodded. "Or it could have been a distraction for something bigger. Consider it done."

Noah hugged his wife close as he watched Leland cross the foyer to the family room. "We'll have to reach out to all the covens and build our own army."

"And stop Khan. But first, we have to find him." Vanessa hugged Noah back and trembled slightly.

He kissed her forehead and said, "You, Kalissa, and Angelica can hold down the fort here; keep the lines of communication open between the covens."

Casting him a narrowed-eyed glare, she asked, "What about you?"

"I will fight if I am needed. Until then, I'll make curses and potions to use as ammo."

Vanessa cupped his cheek in her warm hand. He stared down into chocolate brown eyes with flecks of gold. Sadness mingled with concern and compassion in their depths. She was his world. And had been since they were teens—over three hundred years ago.

A gentle smile formed, but it was the one she used when scolding the children. "As much as I hate the thought of you fighting, risking your life, I want Khan stopped. Enough is enough."

He kissed her mouth and then slid his lips down her jaw to her throat. "I've seen the end of this battle. It's not pretty, but it will end soon."

"No war is pretty."

No, it wasn't. Noah just hoped he could decipher his latest vision in time to stop Khan from destroying the humans.

CHAPTER FOUR

*D*esiree filled her pack with the various items Lex had laid out for her. Things like water, power bars for nourishment, a gun, ammo, and a few jars of potion-filled paintballs. "What's in these?"

Lex answered without looking at her. "Since elemental magic doesn't work in the Underworld, I filled the paintballs with elemental potions. The red balls are fire bombs. Blue ones are ice spells to freeze an opponent long enough to cut their head off. Green are illusion spells meant to make them see their worst fears. They are to be used for distractions."

"Good to know." She carefully placed the containers in her pack. "How long of a trip is it? I mean, time here moves slower. Or is it faster? Anyway, are the rations we have enough?"

"Time moves slower here than the human realm. We can still conjure items here, but we can also hunt for food." Lex swung his pack over his shoulder and faced her.

She scrunched her face, not sure she wanted to eat anything in the Underworld. Ignoring the heat of Lex's stare, she shrugged on her pack and noted that Ryn was ready and waiting by the door. His renewed strength made him appear older in the sense of knowledge and power. However, there was still an aura of sadness and something else darker she couldn't put a finger on around him.

"He doesn't need you to fix him," Lex whispered in her ear, making her jump.

Taking a step away from him, she shrugged. "I can't fix him, but I might know someone who can help him heal."

"You know he's gay, right?"

Desiree rolled her eyes. "Of course, I do. My element is Spirit—the one element that does work in the Underworld."

When they reached Ryn, the demon gave them a raised brow. "You do know I can hear you two, right?" He focused on Desiree and frowned. "I don't need fixing or to be fixed up."

She patted his arm as she exited the house. "You'll thank me later."

"Desiree."

Ryn's growl was interrupted by Lex's laugh. "Dude, there is no use. She's a female with her mind made up."

The sound of Lex's laugh warmed her. It was the first time she'd heard it. From that point, she decided to try and make him laugh more often.

Coming to a stop a few feet from the house, Desiree turned to face the males. "Are we going on foot?" Because she sure didn't see any form of transportation. "Unless we are teleporting. In that case, I need to look at a map to see where I'm going."

She could piggyback off Lex and Ryn, but that would expend too much energy.

"We need to conserve our power in case the natives get stupid." Lex grinned and led the way to a small barn-like building several yards from the house. Inside was a VW Dune Buggy.

"How did you get this here?" Desiree asked, surprised to see a vehicle of any kind on this side. However, the buggy did seem perfect for the dirt roads.

"I brought it over a few pieces at a time so I wouldn't catch Khan's attention." Lex pulled a key from the wall next to the door. "I hope it runs. I haven't started in a couple of years."

Desiree removed her pack and set it on the floor behind the passenger seat. "Might need fresh gas, then."

Nodding, Lex set about draining the fuel and then conjured a few cans with new gas no doubt. Watching him fill the tank, she wondered about what he'd said about conjuring things. "If we can conjure things here, why can't we teleport out? Why did the spirits attack me when I asked them for help?"

Ryn answered her questions. "The Underworld is a parallel reality to the human world, just like the Afterworld. Both have things like motor vehicles and resources like gas. With the portals closed the way they are, it's impossible to conjure something from the human world, but we can conjure from within the Underworld. The spirits are angry because they too are stuck here and unable to roam free from realm to realm."

"I sure hope the oracle can tell us something useful." Desiree climbed into the buggy and waited.

It would be dumb luck if Khan and Samoan were

in the human realm. That thought sent a slice of fear through her. *Mom*. What if Khan's army was there too and attacking the covens and…

Lex's face appeared in her line of sight. His large, warm hands wrapped around her upper arms. "Calm down."

"What if Khan isn't here. I need to get home, check on my mom." A sudden sense of calm fell over her, making it easier for her to breathe.

Meeting Lex's gaze, she noted how the streaks of crimson in his eyes brightened. He stared at her for a few moments. The ability to reach another *magickin's* mind and calm them was something only a magical partner could do.

Lex kissed her forehead, then asked, "Feel better?"

"Yes. Thank you." She meant it. Although it annoyed her to be reminded that she was destined to mate with the Death Demon.

A complication she didn't need.

Lex hated how quietly Desiree sat next to him. Since her panic attack before leaving his house, she hadn't said a word or looked at him. From the way she slouched in the seat, staring out the windshield, he didn't sense any anger, just a hint of sadness mixed with anxiety. Lex wanted nothing more than to turn around and take her back home and keep her safe. While at the same time, he wanted to destroy Khan and Samoan for everything they'd done.

After about another mile of no noise but the tires on the dirt road, Desiree straightened in her seat. From the corner of his eye, he noted how she turned her body slightly in the seat to face him. "My magic depends on the natural world. It scares me to be so weak."

Without conscious thought, he rested a hand on hers and gave a gentle squeeze. "You are not weak."

The sense that she wanted to argue with him drifted along his awareness. Sparing a quick glance to her, he smiled at how she settled back into the slouching position in her seat. If she feared she'd lose her powers, he'd have to reassure her that he wouldn't let that happen. She was his mate.

His to protect.

His to fall in love with.

Only he was already falling. The more time he spent with her, the more he wanted to claim her. The question was, could he entrust his heart to her? There was nothing tying her to him after they got out of the Underworld.

He'd have to woo her. But how?

As if reading his mind, Ryn stuck his head between the seats and said, "You two need some alone time. Have sex. Bond. There is so much sexual tension bouncing between you, it makes my head hurt. So, I'm going to do some snooping around."

In the passenger seat, Desiree tensed. Lex gripped the steering wheel a little tighter. When he glanced to the back seat, Ryn was gone. Teleported to where-the-fuck-ever to do who knew what.

Have sex. Bond.

The demon's words echoed ones that Lex had thought over and over since meeting the sexy strawberry-blond next to him.

"Maybe he's right." Desiree's voice was barely

spoken loud enough to breach the roar of the engine, but Lex heard her loud and clear all the same.

He slammed on the brakes, threw the buggy in park, and turned in his seat to stare at her. "Right about what?"

She returned his gaze with drawn brows and pursed lips. "Sex and bonding. I mean, we are magical partners. Denying that will only add complications to our mission." She lowered her gaze and sagged in the seat. A hint of sadness flowed from her.

Seeing her unhappy or hurt in any way, broke something inside Lex. The protector within him growled, wanting to shelter her from everything that could bring her harm. But the man knew that would only push her away.

Cupping her chin, he gently lifted her gaze back to his. "Say it."

She briefly closed her eyes and let out a sigh. "My powers here are weak. I would only drag you down."

"If we bond, our powers merge." Lex wanted nothing more than to make her his. "I don't want to mate for power or convenience."

Her eyes rounded, and she jerked away from him. "That is not why I offered." She folded her arms. "Just forget it. I'll manage."

There was a hitch in her voice that told him she had been sincere in her proposal to mate. And he'd fucked it up. *Way to go, asshole.*

He started the car, and they drove in silence for a few miles before coming to a cave he'd used before as camp. Back when he used to do Xara's bidding.

When he parked the buggy, Desiree glanced around. "What are we doing?"

"We will camp here and head out at first light."

Reaching the cave entrance, he glanced back at her, still sitting in the car. She didn't look at him as she said, "I don't want to mate anymore. I told you to forget it."

In two long strides, he was at the passenger side of the buggy. He picked her up. "I don't believe you. And from what I understand, Ayden and Kalissa were miserable during the fifteen years they were apart. I found you, and I'm not letting you go. I will make you mine."

CHAPTER FIVE

*D*esiree kicked her legs and wiggled until Lex put her on her feet inside the cave. When he released her, she shoved him away. "I never meant it to sound like I was using you for power."

He stilled and stared at her for several long moments. "I didn't think that at all."

"But you said..." She sagged and wrapped her arms around her middle. "The longer I'm down here, the worse I feel. There is so much negative energy and darkness. It's suffocating."

In a breath of a moment, he stood in front of her. His fingers gently lifted her chin to gaze into his chocolate eyes with their rivers of crimson. His brows were drawn together. To most, he would appear cold, but not to her. Her Divinity gift to touch one's soul or spirit allowed her to see what Lex hid from the world.

And he knew he couldn't hide from her.

No more than she could from him.

"My own mate betrayed my people and me." The red in his eyes brightened as he spoke. Out of instinct, she placed a hand on his cotton-covered chest over his heart and opened herself to him. He drew in a slow, long breath, then released it just as slowly.

"I'm done with betraying my kind." A tear rolled down her cheek.

Lex swiped it away with his thumb. "I want to believe you."

Her heart hurt. What did she expect? For everything to be forgiven with puppies and rainbows? No. Her future was as bleak as the Underworld.

When she stepped back, he gripped her upper arms and held her in place. Her pulse quickened, and she winced. For a moment, she thought he was going to lash out at her. Instead, he kissed her.

His mouth crushed hers in a hot, raw demand for more. His dark power whirled around them, intensifying her need.

Threading her fingers through his shoulder-length hair, she pulled him closer. She needed this.

The closeness, the raw passion he stirred within her. It fueled a hunger deep down that she'd been starving for, for far too long.

He cupped her ass and lifted her off the ground. She wrapped her legs around him, fully aware of his hard length behind his jeans. She fought back a groan when he walked toward the cave wall and pressed her back against it.

Belly burning with need, she bit his lip while sending a thought to him. *"We will be stronger once bound, but it is your choice."*

He broke the kiss and locked gazes with her. There was a slight curiosity in his features. Normally, she wouldn't be able to communicate telepathically with him or any of the Divinities. After all, she didn't share the bond Hecate had placed on them. But Lex was different. They, together, were different.

They were *Porters* and magical partners.

When she'd opened herself to him earlier, it allowed her to connect with him. But only to communicate. Nothing else. He, however, could reach inside her and strip her of everything.

By the hardened stare he gave her, he knew what she'd done. "You place your trust too freely."

"No. Not anymore. I gave my trust to you and

placed my life in your hands. That way, you know I can't hurt you." She cupped his cheek. "You make me want things I've never wanted before. Plus, you make me hope for a brighter future."

He took her hand and placed it on his chest, covering it with his own. Just then, he opened his heart and soul to her. Magic flowed through her, warm and electrifying. "I'm bare to you as you are to me. With the promise to protect and care for you, I open my heart and soul to bond with you as my mate. Do you accept?"

It was the binding of two *Porters*. She'd researched everything about the race since she was a child. One of the most beautiful things about them was their mating rituals. They were different per couple, but the words were very similar. "I accept, and also promise to protect and care for you until death breaks our bond."

She gasped as power slammed into her. Dark, warm, and familiar. Lex's *Porter* magic was similar to hers, but his Death Demon half made it darker, edgier.

Lex snaked an arm around her waist and hugged her to him, their bodies meshing together as if they belonged. Two halves of a whole finally brought together.

When she met his gaze, desire consumed her. *Mine.*

She could get lost in his eyes. Crimson swirled in a sea of chocolate.

He claimed her lips harder than he had the first two kisses. A wildfire brewed as he pushed past her lips to enter her mouth. She twined her tongue with his and moaned.

She gasped as coolness from the stone wall seeped through her cotton T-shirt. Lex thrust his hard thigh between her legs, drawing another moan from her. He deepened the kiss in greedy need. The link from the binding magic, forever linking them together, grew stronger by the moment. She relished the roughness of his touch, loving it. It was as if he knew just what she needed. Maybe he did. They were magical mates.

Fisting her hand in his dark hair, she tugged him closer as she thrust her tongue into his mouth to dance with his. He growled, backed up, and ripped her pants from her body, then lifted her, maneuvering her legs to either side of his waist. Anticipation fluttered inside her. Desire burned within and across her flesh. A moment later, he thrust inside her while breaking the kiss.

She sucked in a breath as he pierced her neck

with his fangs. Pleasurable pain assailed her, making her cry out as he thrust in and out of her. He slipped his hand beneath her T-shirt and cupped her breast, pinching and rolling her taut nipple between his forefinger and thumb. Sparks of desire skidded over her skin and rushed through her blood, making her scream out in release.

The bond took full hold of them both, connecting them for their long existences.

Lex's body tensed a moment before he growled out his own orgasm.

He held her to him for several moments before he pulled out and conjured a small towel and a replacement pair of jeans. Handing the items to her, he stepped back.

There was a long silence between them while Desiree cleaned up and dressed. She wasn't sure what to say. Her body hummed with bliss and the extra power from the bond. His power.

"You are more powerful than you lead everyone to believe."

His words were soft, but there was a growl in his tone. Understanding washed over her. The mistrust directed at her even after she'd opened up to him was because she hadn't been honest about her abilities. With a sigh, she sat with her legs folded on the stone floor. "My *Porter* power is stronger than my Divinity magic. *Porters* are rumored to be dangerous and extinct. From a very young age, my mother taught me to hide that power, lock it away, and never let anyone know just how powerful I was. I should have told you, but I was scared."

He muttered a string of curses barely audible, then sat beside her. "What are you afraid of?"

She shrugged. "At first, I was afraid for Matty's life. Samoan used him to make me do what she wanted. I didn't want her knowing I was stronger than I pretended to be. She would have used it to hurt my son and my coven."

"I feel there is something else."

Desiree closed her eyes briefly, holding back the tears threatening to spill down her cheeks. After taking a deep breath and releasing it slowing, she hugged her waist and told him her darkest secret. "I lied about Matty's father. Well, not completely. He was one of the warlocks I told you about from college. But it wasn't a one-night fling. The three of us became good friends, and I started to fall for them even though neither were my magical partner."

As if sensing her loss, he scooted closer and drew her into his lap. Warmth and acceptance surrounded her, giving her the courage to continue. "Matty's father's name is Stephan, and our third was Daniel. After walking me to my dorm one night, they were attacked by demons and killed. It wasn't until recently that I found out that Samoan had them killed because Stephan was a *Porter*."

"When did you discover this?" Lex kept his tone low, but she felt his trust in her—not that there was much of it to begin with—slipping.

"The day before we came here to rescue Teddy-Bear. Samoan called my cell and left a message, taunting me with how Stephan and Daniel had begged for their lives. And telling me that Mathew looked so much like his father." The tears fell then while rage surged through her veins. "I want Samoan dead. No one should have to suffer any more of her twisted, evil plans."

Lex hugged her tighter and kissed the top of her head. "I promise you, Samoan will get what is coming to her." He sighed and settled back against the cave wall. A moment later, a blanket covered them. "Get some rest. Tomorrow will be a long day on the road. The faster we get to Xara and hopefully get answers, the quicker we can get out of Hell."

She nodded and closed her eyes. Getting out of Hell was a great plan. She needed to get to her mother and their coven to see if everyone was okay.

Lex squeezed her gently, again. "Shh. Sleep."

A smile tugged at her lips. It was going to take a lot to get used to having the Death Demon tuned to her emotions. But she wouldn't hide them from him. She needed him to trust her. Trust that she'd never betray him as his former mate had.

CHAPTER SIX

*S*amoan fingered the smoky quartz wrapped in silver wire and strung on a black leather cord. Sparks of silver and gold bounced within the stone—the dark magic from the Dark Divine. She'd done it. With Mathew's help.

The kid didn't even know what he'd done. She'd asked him to transfer the dark power to the stone, telling him the Dark Divine had volunteered to help them win the war.

He did it with ease, which had surprised Samoan. She'd apparently underestimated his abilities.

Focusing on the stone, she called out to the Dark Divine connected to the demonic version of the Sinew. Within moments, several of the witches appeared, awaiting their orders. A smile lifted her lip, and she filled with pride. Pointing to the four closest to her, she commanded, "Go to the Town-center and make yourselves known. Use your powers to shake up the humans. I don't care what you do. Just make it big enough that the Divinities will have to come and shut it down."

The four nodded and dematerialized. She turned to the others and said, "You will prepare for the grand finale, the end of the Divinities."

Zach entered Ayden's office at the Maxville Sher-iff's office when the call came in. Four witches were at the Towncenter, using magic to destroy cars and stores. He and Ayden didn't waste time jumping in Zach's car, placing a cloaking spell over it, and tele-porting to the large, outdoor mall.

Once they'd materialized behind one of the stores, Zach sent a telepathic message to Lydia and the other Divinities. "Got trouble at the Towncenter."

Zach himself wasn't telepathic. He possessed the ability to communicate only with the Divinities he was linked to through Hecate.

Lydia was the first to flash in. A moment later, Khloe and then Jagger materialized. Khloe was the first to ask, "What's going on?"

Ayden grunted and said, "Dark Divine. But why would they tear up the mall?"

"I smell a trap," Jagger growled and moved toward the front of the buildings. "My bet is that Samoan is somehow controlling them."

Zach and the others followed. "That would mean she succeeded in creating the Dark Sinew." If that were the case, then they were definitely walking into a trap. *Fun times*. "Just look out for demons to pop in at any moment."

"Try not to kill the Dark Divine. They are victims in this, too." Lydia fell into step with Zach and Ayden.

Khloe nodded as if agreeing with Lydia. "True, but it'll be hard not to if they were commanded to kill us."

Fuck. The whole thing was screwed up. "To kill or not to kill. Samoan must think she has us by the nads. Okay, we kill the demons and knock out the Dark Divine."

Just then, a half-dozen demons materialized in the parking lot. When they made eye contact with Zach and the others, they charged forward. Jagger and Khloe went off in opposite directions. Ayden charged in, throwing energy balls as he went. That left Lydia and Zach in the middle.

Casting Lydia a sideways smirk, Zach said, "You want to go bowling?"

She smiled, showing the points of fangs and damn if he didn't get hard. "I'd love to."

Zach formed a basketball-sized energy ball while she formed a fireball of equal size. Together, they thrust them into the charging demons. Right before the ball hit the demons, they merged, flashing bright orange and red. The demons' screams died within moments after being consumed by the mixture of magic and fire.

Then there were three. Another couple of screams sounded.

"Correction, one to go." Lydia laughed, reading Zach's thoughts. As a mated pair, nothing was a secret.

Zach would have it no other way.

He glanced up in time to see the last demon dematerialize. "Coward."

Scanning the mall parking lot, he didn't see the Dark Divine either. Fear cut into his gut. The whole fight had been too easy. As if the demons were only a distraction. Dread burned his insides, and he locked gazes with Ayden.

"Kalissa says everything is good there." Ayden drew his brows together.

"What is it?" Khloe and Zach said at the same time.

"Sindee feels Samoan calling to her. Lydia, you'll need to put her out until we find a way to break the control the demoness has over the Dark Divine."

Lydia frowned. Through their magical bond, Zach felt her sadness at having to do so. He reached out and linked his fingers with hers. Then Ayden said, "It is at Sindee's request. She'd never be able to live with herself if she hurt anyone."

Nodding, Lydia released a sigh. "I know. Let's get home and prepare for another round. I hope Papa can assemble an army soon. We're going to need all the help we can get."

This battle was only a small taste of what the crazy bitch, Samoan, was up to.

Desiree wasn't sure what she'd expected the home of a dragon oracle to look like, but a single-family style cottage wasn't it. Weren't dragons huge?

Just then, she caught a glimpse of two pseudo dragons playing in the backyard. They took off running, then soared through the air toward them. Desiree smiled at their red and purple scales with a shimmer of gold that caught the dim light of the Underworld.

Once they noticed her and Lex, the dragons stopped playing and hovered in the air a few feet away. They stared for a few moments, then turned around and yelled, "Xara," while flying to the front door.

The door opened before the small dragons reached it. They darted inside, and out came a tall redhead with modest curves and few clothes, not leaving much to the imagination. "Hello, Lex, I've been waiting for you."

A spike of jealousy raced through Desiree's veins. "I thought you said she was a dragon," she gritted out between her teeth.

Lex grunted before saying, "She is." Then he stepped forward a few steps. "Xara, I don't have to tell you that I don't have time for pleasantries."

The redhead rolled her eyes. "I understand the urgency. What about payment?"

"You have my word that I will return."

Just then, a flash rippled in the irises of her purple dragon eyes. A smile lifted her lips. "On second thought, completing your mission will be payment enough. Kahn is bound to the Underworld. It is the way of the ruler. His mate, however, is not. She has the dark crystal and controls the army from above."

Desiree's heart sped up, and she moved to stand beside Lex. "How can we stop her?"

Xara slowly moved her gaze to Desiree. "You will know when it is time to do so. Until then, the two of you must stay safe."

"Is that all you can tell us?" Annoyance rode Desiree, fueling her frustration all the more. There has to be more. When she stepped forward, Lex gripped her arm, stopping her.

Xara was inches from Desiree in a flash, her eyes

showing her dragon. Then the pupils elongated into vertical slits while the irises darkened to a deep violet. "You will need your bravado to save everything you hold dear. I cannot tell you what I see because I fear it would change too much of the future. But I can tell you, whatever you do, don't turn your back on Samoan, and when you have the chance, kill her."

The words, *before it's too late*, drifted in Desiree's mind. Whether the dragon had sent the thought or Desiree added them, she didn't know.

A moment later, Xara took Desiree's hand and held it palm up. Desiree tried to jerk it from the dragon's grip, but it was no use. She was too strong. Then Xara placed a silver-dollar-size, oval moonstone in Desiree's palm and curled her fingers around it.

Without letting go, Xara leaned in to whisper in her ear. "Use the stone to call upon the moon for strength." Xara glanced to Lex and frowned. A shadow of something Desiree swore was sadness passed over her features. But it was gone almost as fast as it appeared.

Xara stepped back. "I'm sorry I can't give you any more information. I fear your trip here was a waste."

In a puff of purple smoke, Xara shifted into a

four-foot-tall dragon. Her scales matched the color of her eyes with silver lining the edges of each scale. She stepped off the porch, forcing Lex and Desiree to move out of her way. Extending her wings, she jumped into the air and took flight.

Desiree crossed her arms. "That *was* a waste of time." Lex shook his head and stalked back to the buggy. Desiree jogged after him. "She didn't even tell us how to get out of here."

"Get in. We obviously can get out. We just need to figure out how."

After climbing into the car, she stared at him. "That doesn't help."

He dropped his shoulders and faced her, taking her hand in his. "We will figure it out. There has to be something we missed."

"Yeah, like the memo to get the hell out before the portals locked down."

Desiree got out of the buggy and slowly made her way into the house. Before opening the door, she caught movement to her right. A familiar magic drifted in the air. *Matty.*

She rushed down the steps and met his stare from the woods. "I'd like to talk to you. I'm not going to hurt you."

He didn't move or speak.

Desiree wanted to cry, scream, flash over to him and make him listen. Yet, she couldn't do any of those things. She was a stranger to him. The mother who'd turned him over to the demons.

A sob lodged in her throat. She felt Lex hover near the door, their new bond making her fully aware of the Death Demon's every move. *Just as he feels my pain right now.* "Mathew, I would never have abandoned you. Samoan lied. To me, to you."

Still, he didn't move. What else could she say to get through to him? Her heart ached more by the moment. "Please, I love you. I only wanted to protect you."

He frowned then. Maybe it was the crack in her voice as she pled, trying so hard not to burst into sobs. "Matty, I thought you were dying. Samoan said she'd heal you…"

Her heart stilled for a moment as Mathew

stepped from the tree line. Then his gaze jerked to Lex behind her, and he vanished.

She whirled around and faced Lex. His drawn brows and half-smile stopped her from yelling at him. "What?"

"He is not bound to the Underworld."

"Huh?" She didn't understand what he was talking about.

Lex looked at her then. "Mathew. He didn't just teleport away, he left the Underworld altogether. Did you not see it?"

Glancing to the space where Mathew had stood moments ago, Desiree shook her head. "No." She'd been too focused on getting her son to talk to her.

"He can freely move between the worlds even with it on lockdown."

He was basically a full-blood *Porter*. Of course, he could... But she and Lex could not. Mathew wasn't a witch—at least not since his transformation —so Hecate didn't have power over him. And neither did Khan because Mathew wasn't a demon either.

Returning her attention back to Lex, she asked, "What are you thinking?"

Lex turned and disappeared inside the house. She followed. The demon was up to something. And she'd find out what. Especially if it concerned her son.

"Lex, answer me."

He faced her then, stopping in the middle of the living room. "Sorry. My theory is that we may be able to piggyback off Mathew's power the next time he leaves."

Fury flowed red-hot, boiling Mathew's blood as he flung the door to Samoan's apartment open. It crashed into the wall. Samoan sat on the couch with her laptop on her jean-covered thighs. She didn't look at him when she spoke. "Where have you been?"

"Around." He advanced toward her, needing answers. "Who is Desiree?"

Samoan's fingers stilled briefly over the keyboard. "She's a Divinity currently trapped in the Underworld."

He walked to her and knocked the laptop from her lap, sending it flying across the living room. "Who is she to *me*?"

Samoan's cobalt blue eyes met his, her brows bunched into an angry line, and her lips curled. "She is nothing. A mother who gave away her child because he was turning...and these are her words... 'into a monster.'"

She was lying. Mathew saw it then. The same twitch in the muscle under her right eye. It was slight, but he caught it that time. "I don't believe you anymore."

"I see." Samoan stood and collected her computer. Carrying it to the dining room table, she continued speaking. "You've been talking with the witch. How are you sure she isn't using you to get to me?"

Was the demoness serious? Mathew may only be ten years old, but he was smart. He'd finished his high school education a few months ago. Plus, he'd studied anything he could about history—both human and *magickin*—and he was more powerful than Samoan. Only he didn't let the bitch who'd raised him know that.

He'd never call Samoan "mother" because, well, she'd never been one to him. There was no maternal instinct there. No love. Just cold demands. He believed she was incapable of loving anyone.

Mathew, on the other hand, had a heart. He'd dreamt of the day when he'd find his birth mother and be loved.

Deep down, he knew Desiree was who she said. His inhuman senses from being a changeling and a *Porter* allowed him to recognize that she was being truthful with him. However, Samoan had brainwashed him his whole life. Telling him his real mother had given him away, not wanting to see him ever again. And then telling him she was dead.

"She wouldn't have to use me," he muttered and moved closer to Samoan to see what was so important on the computer that had her so preoccupied. A satellite map of Jacksonville was on the screen.

When he glanced at her again, he saw it. The large smoky quartz hanging from her neck. The stone held the magic of the Dark Divine. What was she doing with it?

Samoan lifted her gaze to his and smiled. "The stone will aid me in leading the Divinities into a trap. They want to protect the humans and *magickin*. Their bleeding hearts for humanity will be their end. Plus, the stone keeps the Dark Divine army under my control."

He froze. No. When she'd asked him to help transfer the power to the stone, she'd said that the Dark Divine had volunteered; that they were helping them to assist the Divinities. Samoan was crazy. Totally and utterly insane.

She never meant to aid the Divinities. However, he'd figured that out months ago. What could he do?

With the Divinities down three members, they were weaker than as a full unit. Kalissa was pregnant, and Lex and Desiree were trapped in the Underworld—at least until Mathew got them out.

With a new purpose, he turned toward the door. He ignored Samoan when she asked where he was going.

She'd find out soon enough. He could do something about Samoan's and Khan's evil plans.

The Divinities would once again have eight members on the front line. And an army at their back.

CHAPTER SEVEN

$\mathcal{L}$ex paced in front of the fireplace as he, Ryn and Desiree brainstormed on how to get the fuck out of Hell. There had to be a way he and Des could combine their *Porter* power to get out.

"What did Xara mean by 'the way of the ruler?'"

Ryn answered before Lex could respond. "It's like a magical code of conduct to keep the balance."

Desiree scrunched up her nose and frowned. "Isn't that what he wants? To break down the veils between the three worlds?"

Stopping his route, he met Desiree's stare. "Yes, but there are unwritten and unspoken rules in doing so. If he just left the Underworld and disrupted the balance, he'd be without an advantage."

"I'm not following you. Breaking out would unleash an apocalyptic event. He would have what he wants—Hell on Earth." Desiree glanced to Ryn then back to Lex. Her green eyes sparked with worry and fear.

"If Khan was to break out of Hell, the gods would come to Earth also. He'd be outnumbered, and the humans would be no more." Ryn spoke in a calm, low tone. However, Lex heard the tremor in his voice.

Desiree's eyes widened. "I didn't think of that. The gods would be forced to wipe everyone out. Reset humanity."

Lex shrugged. "Something like that. Khan doesn't want the gods involved, so he's building armies and sending out his minions."

Desiree fell silent as if taking in the information. "Wait. What about the attacks on the Maxville Coven over three centuries ago? He was there."

"And Hecate was free to stop him. Khan found a way out without throwing off the balance. Most likely, he used a human soul to do it. That night, Hecate gifted the Divinities with their powers and linked the Elders together." Lex stilled at the sudden surge of power filling the room. Someone was there.

He moved to the front door as a knock sounded.

Yanking it open, he froze. Mathew stood on the other side, jaw working and brows drawn together as if pissed off about something. Lex raised his own brow. "Ready to talk?"

"Samoan is a lying bitch."

"Yep." Lex stepped aside to allow Mathew to enter.

Entering the living room, Lex watched Desiree closely. She stood, and tears filled her eyes. Unable to stand the heartache flowing through their bond, Lex closed the distance between them. He took her hand in his.

Mathew glanced at their linked hands and then met Lex's gaze. "Are you my father?"

"No." Lex answered simply, then waited for Desiree to fill in the rest.

Desiree trembled at Lex's side as she spoke. "Your father's name was Stephan. He was a warlock and a *Porter*, and one of the two men I was in love with in college. We weren't magical mates, but we did love each other. And then both he and Daniel were taken from me. By Samoan. I was... The demoness used me and then lied to get me to hand you over. I thought you were ill and dying. I would have never let her take you if I'd known the truth."

With a sob, Mathew ran to her, wrapping his

arms around her in a tight hug. Desiree burst into tears and hugged him back. Lex's own heart melted at the reunion. Yet guilt and sorrow still filled Desiree's heart.

After several moments, Mathew pulled back and said, "I can get you out of here. Samoan has the Dark Sinew and control of the Dark Divine army. She plans to trap the Divinities in one place to destroy them."

"Then let's get out."

With a nod, Mathew waved a hand and opened a portal. Then he motioned for them to go. Lex grabbed Desiree's hand, pushed Ryn through the portal first, and then entered it with his mate. They exited a few yards from the back porch of the Divinity House.

A moment later, Mathew materialized beside them. "Looks like no one is home."

"They're most likely at the Maxville Coven." Lex advanced to the gatehouse while sending Jagger a telepathic message. *"Jag, we're at the Divinity House."*

"Thank fuck. We're on our way."

Damn, it was good to hear his brother's voice.

A moment later, Jagger, Khloe, Zach, and Lydia materialized a few feet away. Jagger crossed the short distance and drew Lex into a hug. With a heavy sigh, Lex let down what was left of the walls around his heart and squeezed Jagger back. A sense of family and unconditional love surrounded them.

Pulling out of the embrace, Jagger met Lex's gaze. "It's good to have you back."

Even though Lex could sense that his brother was glad and relieved to see him, there was a dark feeling of dread hovering over him, as well. "What is it?"

"Samoan has the Dark Sinew."

"Yes, we know." Lex studied his brother for several moments. "And?"

Jagger stepped aside and motioned for them to come in. Once inside, Lex's brother led them to the family room. "Samoan can also control the Dark Divine."

Desiree hugged her waist beside Lex. "We know that, too."

"Ayden and the others will be here shortly. Ayd is arguing with Lissa about fighting in the war." Zach turned.

Lex frowned. "She doesn't want him to fight?" He could understand it since they'd spent fifteen years apart because of a memory spell. Besides, the female was pregnant and probably suffering high anxiety with everything going on.

A laugh drew his attention to Khloe. "No. Lissa may be the docile twin, but she's just as stubborn as I am. Besides, she's like a mama bear. Wants to protect all those she's claimed as hers. So Ayden is trying to talk her into staying at Maxville."

With everyone gathered in the living room, Jagger nodded to Mathew, and Lex shifted closer to the kid in a protective manner. Desiree's anxiety was making Lex twitchy. With everyone on edge, Lex wanted to get out of there, but they needed to finish this, end the war once and for all.

At least end Kahn's reign in the Underworld.

Rolling his eyes, Jagger talked to the boy. "What do you know about Samoan's plan?"

Mathew straightened his spine. "Samoan will use the Dark Sinew to control the Dark Divine and use them like an army. She said she would also use the humans and *magickin* to lead you into a trap where she'll kill you."

The kid shivered as if a chill had rippled up his spine. Lex stopped himself from reaching out to comfort him. Would Mathew accept his compassion if he did?

Zach cursed as he flopped down on the sofa and propped his sneakers on the coffee table. "She didn't happen to tell you how she was going to trap us, did she?"

"No. Samoan is clever that way. She never shares what she is up to. Only what she wants you to know." Mathew shifted from foot to foot.

Lex touched his arm. When the kid glanced up at him, Lex motioned to the chair in front of them. With a short nod, Mathew sat. Relief rolled off the boy, but he didn't relax. Letting a low growl rumble from deep within, Lex spoke. "Samoan needs to be stopped. I say we set a little trap of our own."

CHAPTER EIGHT

"*I* don't know where I fit in."

Desiree turned at Mathew's soft-spoken words as she stepped out onto the back porch. He sat on the top step, looking out into the backyard.

Inhaling the cool, clean air, Desiree advanced forward and then sat on the step next to him. "Neither do I. Until recently, I worked alone to try and spoil Samoan's plans. I didn't believe the other Divinities would trust me to fight by their sides."

From the corner of her eye, she caught her son's stare. "What do you mean?"

Breathe. Don't start tearing up. "Samoan used you to get me to help her. Which I pretended not to be able to do. She once had a small piece of Hecate's

Sinew—the one that holds the magic of the three worlds and of *magickin*. She wanted me to charge it. She hoped it would be as powerful as the original."

He stiffened beside her. "Did you do it?"

"No. I got pissed at her, tired of being lied to and used, so I shattered it. Right in front of her." Desiree tugged her sweater tighter around herself. "That was when I called Lex for help and confessed what I'd done."

"You didn't charge it, so you didn't do anything wrong." There was a catch in his voice.

"Before that, I had given her information on the Divinities. Especially after the Sinew was found and brought here. I was the one who told her there were Dark Divine in my coven. It was my fault that my home was attacked." A tear slid down her cheek.

Mathew scooted closer to her so their arms touched. "I moved the Dark Divine power into the Dark Sinew."

"I guessed as much." There was no judgment in her tone. Why would she judge him? They were both traitors to their kind. Yet the Divinities had done nothing but accept her into their circle.

Silence settled between mother and son for several long moments. In a way, it was nice. Just sitting in the cool, late morning.

"What will they do with me?"

Desiree jerked her gaze to him. "What do you mean?"

"I am the reason Samoan has control of the Dark Divine and their power. I committed a crime." Mathew's blue eyes shone with unshed tears.

Movement at the door caught Desiree's attention as Lydia exited the house followed by Khloe. Both women sat on the wood floor of the porch. Desiree and Mathew turned to them, and Lydia held out a hand. "I'm Lydia."

Mathew glanced to Desiree as if unsure before shaking Lydia's hand. "You're a healer." He narrowed his gaze and frowned. "And a cursed vampire."

Lydia laughed. "Yes. Samoan finds ways to amuse herself."

A *pfft* from Khloe drew their attention. The tips of her white-blonde hair were purple instead of the usual pink. "Samoan is crazy and must die." She extended her hand to Mathew. "I'm Khloe."

"A shifter." Mathew smiled.

Khloe leaned in and returned his smile. "You're a changeling. We'll have to go hunting together sometime."

"I don't hunt meat. But I could run with you on the full moon."

Khloe perked up. "Deal. Now, about your punishment."

Hot dread burned Desiree's gut. Before she could grab Mathew, Khloe caught her wrist. Then she looked at Mathew, held out her hand, and conjured a tray with four cups and a container of cream. "Hot chocolate."

Relief hit Desiree in a wave. She slid her hand to Khloe's and squeezed. The Divinity sighed. "Look. We've all done things that suck. Des, you tried to hurt Samoan's plans more than you helped. You didn't have a choice."

Lydia spoke next. "As a mother, I understand why you thought you had to do what you did. That alone is why Hecate didn't strip you of your powers." She glanced to Mathew. "You were an innocent in all of this. Taken from your mom as a toddler and raised with demons. Samoan probably fed you garbage about how you would be helping the worlds."

"She assumed the Divinities were out to destroy her and her mate." Mathew snorted and added, "Which isn't wrong. But she believed she was making a better place to live."

Ha. Desiree fisted her hands. "The bitch is crazy. It would be a better place for her and her minions."

Khloe nodded. "True, true. But it's not like we

can go back in time and change things. We have to go with the hand we are dealt and go from there."

"I can."

They all stared at Mathew. Desiree asked, "Can what?"

Mathew smiled. "Go back in time. With your and Lex's help, a small group of us can go back and fix this."

Desiree stared at him with interest. In theory, Mathew could do it. He was, after all, a full-blooded *Porter* and his power was unlike anything she'd felt. However, time travel went beyond portal hopping. "How? I mean, that would take an incredible amount of power and energy."

"Whatever Samoan did to me to transform me into a changeling made my power stronger." Mathew glanced down at his hands in his lap.

Reaching over and covering his hands, Desiree asked, "Have you done it before?"

A slow nod of his head was her answer. Good gods. They could go back and stop it all. But at what expense? Could they truly alter history to save the future?

"I think it's worth talking to Noah about," Khloe offered.

Desiree nodded. Yes, they needed the Elder's insight. As a seer, he'd know better than they would.

The idea was crazy enough to work. Or it could fuck things up worse than they already were.

Lex studied the kid, who looked uneasy with the attention he drew. After making the announcement that he could time jump, the females brought him inside, and Khloe set up the video conferencing for Noah's insight on time travel.

"How far back can you go?" Lex asked.

Mathew met his stare and shrugged. "Not sure. Never purposely tried it, really."

Narrowing his gaze, Lex worked his jaw, his patience running thin. They needed to get to Samoan before she released her army.

Next to him, Desiree placed a hand on his arm. Instantly, he calmed. "You said you time traveled before."

"Yes, once, by accident. A few years ago. I got mad at Samoan for punishing a *Lackey* teen for stealing bread. I just wished I could go back in time and save him from the beating. The next moment, I appeared next to him a few moments before he took the bread." Mathew shuddered. "I believe I can go back and destroy the stone they are using for the Dark Sinew. But I don't know how far back I can go because I've never tested it."

Everyone looked at Noah on the TV monitor. The Elder tapped his finger on the arm chair of his recliner. "Time travel is tricky. Anything you change will affect the future. It's hard to pick the time to jump to. Everything happens for a reason."

Zach Nodded. "Our alternative is to go with the plan to lure Samoan into her own trap. If that backfires, then we'll go back."

"Then we could get stuck in a cycle of trying to fix mistakes and never get anywhere." Noah shook his head. "Well planned, the time travel could work. But you need to make sure you don't interfere with anything but the objective."

Lex sighed. "Only change what we absolutely want to be changed. So we can't go back too far. Less impact on the future."

"I agree," Ayden said as he sat down next to Zach.

"I personally want to see where she is headed with her plan. Lure her into a trap. Then, if we can, take her out. Use the time travel as a last resort."

"If my visions become reality, we may have to go with plan B." Noah sighed. The Elder looked tired, like he hadn't slept for days. Maybe weeks.

Once the video feed had been turned off, Ayden spoke to no one in particular. "Papa's dreams are filled with visions of an apocalypse. He won't go into details with any of us. I'm guessing he doesn't want to shift our focus."

Khloe placed a hand on her brother-in-law's shoulder as if lending him support while leaning into Jagger. "I feel something dark coming. But I agree with Papa. What do we fix if we don't know what to fix?"

Lex caught Desiree slipping out of the room, so he took that opportunity to get her alone to talk. He followed her to the kitchen table in front of a double window looking out into the backyard. "Are you okay?"

She glanced at him and offered a weak smile. "I need to call my mom, but don't know what to say to her."

Longing to be close to her family slammed into his awareness. Taking her hand, he tugged her to a stand and kissed her quickly on the lips. "Call her and tell her you are on your way with a surprise."

She stepped into him and hugged him tightly. "I lied to them."

He placed an index finger under her chin and lifted her gaze to his. "I may have only met your mother briefly, but she has a forgiving soul."

A small smile formed. "She does. Will you come with me?"

"I wouldn't have it any other way."

CHAPTER NINE

*D*esiree wiped her clammy hands on her jeans after she, Lex, and Mathew materialized in her Oceanway Coven home. She'd chosen her home first because she didn't want anyone but her mom to see Mathew. In case his dark presence disturbed some of the residents.

Gods, I'm going to be ill. Her stomach felt as if there were a million butterflies fighting for real estate.

If she were honest with herself, it wasn't Mathew's changeling or dark powers that worried her. It was facing her mother after lying to her and the whole coven for eight years. Telling them Mathew had died from an illness he didn't have.

Before leaving the Divinity House, she'd called her mom and asked her to meet. Knowing her mom, she would be earlier than the ten minutes Desiree had stated.

A light knock sounded on the door. Desiree's heart rate sped up. Lex framed her face in his warm, large hands. "It will be okay."

When she nodded, he placed a tender kiss on her lips and then stepped aside for her to answer the door.

The worst that could happen was her mother asking her to leave the coven. She guessed she could live in the Underworld with Lex. Or get them a place on the river. Maybe the same building where Khloe and Zach had their condos.

"Are you going to let your mother in?"

Lex's low-toned whisper in her ear snapped her out of her thoughts. Taking a breath, she moved to the door, exhaling as she opened it. "Hi, Mom."

Eleese raised her brows, then glanced over her shoulder to Lex. A frown formed but quickly disappeared. Damn. Another secret. Well, her mating Lex wasn't a secret. She just hadn't had the opportunity to tell her mother.

"Please, come in. There is so much I need to tell you."

"Yes, but Noah kept me up-to-date on the war and you and Lex being trapped in the Underworld."

Her mom stepped inside then tugged her into a tight hug. "I thought I'd lost you."

There was a sob in her voice, triggering Desiree's own waterworks. Tears rolled down her cheeks, and she hugged her mom back and inhaled her rosemary scent. "I'm so sorry."

Eleese pulled out of the embrace and searched her face. "No matter what you did, I will still love you."

Desiree nodded and led her mother into the living room. Mathew sat on the window seat facing the back yard. His head lifted from the book in his hand and he stared at Eleese. A knowing flashed in his wild gaze as he stood, setting the book carefully on the seat.

Desiree's mom gasped and covered her mouth, tears welling up in her eyes. "Is this…Mathew?"

"It is, Mama. Samoan…she took him. I lied, and Samoan took him." A sob escaped her.

Lex wrapped his arms around her and held her close. "Samoan used and manipulated Desiree to steal Mathew from her."

Mathew spoke next. "Samoan told me my family was dead. That I was an orphan."

Eleese held out a hand. "The last time I saw you, you were two, and very ill."

"Please, let's sit down." Lex motioned to the sofa and chair around a glass coffee table.

Desiree and her mom nodded and took a seat on the sofa. Mathew seemed uneasy. However, when Desiree patted the seat next to her, he smiled and sat down.

Covering his hand with hers, Desiree told her mother the whole story from the time she'd met Samoan to when Desiree first saw Mathew in the Underworld. When she was done talking, she felt lighter, as if spilling the secrets she'd carried for so long had finally lifted some weight off her; no more lies weighing her down.

Her mom turned sideways on the sofa and cupped Desiree's face. "I wish you would have come to me sooner. Especially about Mathew's father being a *Porter*."

"There was nothing you could have done. Nothing anybody could do."

"Not true. Sometimes, when a child is born with a mix of powerful genes—in this case, a mother who is a Divinity-*Porter* mix and a warlock father who was also a *Porter*—then the powers within will fight each other for dominance." Eleese kissed Desiree on the forehead, then sat back before continuing. "You never went through the power struggle. I figured your *Porter* side wasn't strong enough to matter since your father was only a quarter."

Lex nodded from the chair across from them. "But with Desiree's Divine gift to connect to the spirit world, mixed with the element of Spirit, her *Porter* half would see no reason to fight. It would work together with her Divine power. That's why she is so powerful."

Meeting her mate's stare, Desiree almost laughed. One side of his mouth twisted as if he fought a smile. His eyes held some kind of pride in them. Like the light bulb had flicked on. "I never thought of it like that." She faced her mom again. "So, Mathew wasn't dying due to the transformation. His *Porter* half was fighting him."

Her mom smiled widely and reached a hand across Desiree to Mathew. "He did transform."

"Into a changeling," Desiree added.

Eleese winced and groaned. "I hate that word. It's what the demons used to call shapeshifting witches. It's meant to be an insult. The cursed child left in place of another." She rolled her eyes and leaned into Desiree while squeezing Mathew's hand. "He's a shifter, like me."

Mathew gasped. "You can take any form?"

"Yes. It is my Divine gift."

"Cool. I've never met anyone like me." Mathew scooted closer, sandwiching Desiree between him and her mom.

After a moment, Eleese stood and asked Mathew, "Would you like a tour of the coven? That way, you can familiarize yourself. Oh, and see the school."

Mathew stood, a wide smile on his face. "I'd love to. But I finished high school classes a few months ago."

"You did?" Desiree and Eleese said at the same time.

"Yep. Online classes. You know, the virtual school."

Desiree frowned even though she was happy that he was so bright. While at the same time, he was so much older in experiences than any *magickin* kid his age. "Matty, when this is over, I promise you will learn to be a kid. You'll make friends, laugh, play, and get into trouble."

Her son laughed and launched himself at her, hugging her tightly around the waist. With a heavy heart and tears in her eyes, Desiree hugged him back and kissed the top of his head.

After a few moments, he looked up at her. "I think I'm going to like it here."

"I hope you do. Now, go get to know your grandma."

"Thank you." He squeezed her one more time before leaving with her mom.

Lex stood and moved behind her. He brushed her hair from her neck and placed a kiss on the tender curve to her shoulder. "Someone needs to release some bottled up energy."

His low growl made her weak in the knees. Her sex throbbed with need. Turning in his arms, she captured his mouth in a demanding kiss. He returned it, matching the raw command. His fingers gripped her ass and dug into her cheeks.

When his tongue ran across the seam of her lips, she opened and welcomed the invasion. One of his fangs pricked her tongue, and the sweet tang of her blood in his mouth was oddly arousing.

She ran her hand under his shirt and over the hard, ridged muscles of his chest. A groan escaped him as he pulled back from the kiss, yanked the shirt over his head, and tossed it to the floor.

Passion heated her from the inside out as she took in his creamed-coffee-colored skin tone. Reaching out again, she traced a finger down his chest to the top of his jeans. When she fingered the button, he grabbed her hand and jerked her arm behind her back. His clasp was firm but not painful. It did, however, keep her from touching him.

Suddenly, they were in her bed. Teleported by the Death Demon. Her mate.

She smiled at the latter.

Lex was the last person she'd imagined herself with, but here they were. Mated, and she was falling for him. With everything going on, she wasn't sure when it had happened.

He lowered his body onto hers, pinning her in place.

His hard length pressed into her through their jeans. She moaned out a plea. The ache to have him inside her grew stronger.

Warm breath glided over her skin as he trailed light kisses down her throat, over her shoulder blades, and further. In the next moment, her clothes vanished. She gasped when he took a nipple into his mouth. Hot need shot straight to her core, causing the walls of her sex to pulse.

Oh, gods.

When his tongue flicked the hardened bud, she fisted the sheet and rubbed her throbbing pussy against his erection, still encased in denim. *Damn it.* Unclenching the sheet, she slid one hand between them to unbutton his jeans.

Lex raised his head and seized her wrist. Her heart skipped a beat at the fierce desire showing in his gaze. "I want to fuck you slow and hard. Yet, I will not last." His tone was low and graveled.

She'd take it either way. If she didn't get the release her body screamed for, she wouldn't be held responsible for her actions. "Fast at first. Then round two can be as slow as you want."

The wicked grin on her demon's face was her answer.

She didn't have time to respond with a sassy comeback before his mouth was on hers, his tongue thrusting inside, searching for hers. Her moan changed to a gasp as the rest of his clothes disappeared, and his cock slid inside her.

He stopped halfway in and broke the kiss. Their eyes locked on one another's. A tic formed in his jaw as if he were trying to fight for control. After a brief silence, he thrust in the rest of the way, filling her. She was lost. Lost in the sensation of being consumed and taken by Lex, again.

She wrapped her legs around his waist and moved in sync with his gentle thrusting. With her tongue, she drew his earlobe into her mouth and gently bit down. A growl rumbled from his chest, and he quickened his pace.

Pleasure built from within the depths of her being until her climax threw her over the edge, ripping a scream of pleasure from her. Lex followed her with his own release.

She was boneless as Lex rolled them to the side without pulling out. He hugged her close and fell silent. Her heart stuttered a few beats. Dread ate at her nerves, and the fear of rejection hung close by.

After several long moments, he said, "You make me feel things I don't understand. But I do know I can't let you go."

Relief flooded her, and she snuggled into him. It was close enough to telling her that he was falling for her. She'd take it. At least for now.

She'd take him any way she could.

"I'm addicted to you. There's no getting rid of me now."

He pushed deeper inside her, and she moaned, moving her hips. "Good."

CHAPTER TEN

Mathew burst through the front door of Samoan's downtown apartment and flopped down on her sofa. She was there. He could sense her moving around in her bedroom.

Lying to her wasn't a problem. Trying to hide his emotions would be. Samoan's keen senses were better than anyone Matt knew. Plus, the demoness was smart. However, she would make a mistake. He was going to try and make sure she did tonight.

"How did your visit with your mommy go?"

He held in a growl and clenched his jaw. *Breathe. Don't show her emotion.* "I came here to give you a heads up that they are planning a trap for you."

She raised a brow as she advanced into the living room. "I'm listening."

"I'm supposed to get you to Friendship Fountain, where they will be waiting for you with the Sinew." Mathew yawned as if bored. Actually, he was scared to death.

"Hmm." She sat in the chair across from him, crossed her legs, and bounced one of them vigorously. "Why should I believe you?"

He shrugged. "Don't. I could care less. Desiree isn't the loving mother I hoped she was." On that statement, he allowed some of his emotions loose. "But you can head them off by catching them at the Divinity House. But I'd hurry. They're getting ready to head to the fountain."

She tapped her fingers on the chair arms and studied him for what seemed like ten minutes, maybe longer. Suddenly, she stood and left without a word.

Once he'd felt Samoan leave the building, he sent Desiree a telepathic message. *"She bought it and is on her way."*

"Thank you," Desiree replied. Her voice was sad and anxious at the same time. He closed his eyes. Spending the day and night with his new family had confused him. How was he supposed to act? Just accept them? He wasn't sure who to trust. Even

though he'd place his life in Desiree's hands before Samoan's any day.

The longing for a mother to hug him, love him, outweighed any common sense he may have. So he'd stick around Desiree for the time being.

He hoped she didn't turn out to be another disappointment in his short life.

Desiree steeled her spine and met Lex's gaze. "She's coming."

Khloe stormed by them with Jagger, Zach, and Lydia on her heels—all heading for the front door. "She's here."

Confused, Desiree glanced back to Lex. He gave a jerky nod. "The wards are linked to the Divinities, as well as Jag and me."

He exited the house, and Desiree inhaled slowly, calling her power to the surface. On the exhale, she centered herself. A moment passed before she followed the others outside.

Dark energy flowed all around them. The hairs on her arms and the back of her neck stood on end as Samoan materialized a few yards from the house. The demoness laughed, the sound raking across Desiree's skin. "I see the boy has chosen his side."

Hot fear sliced across Desiree's gut. Where was Mathew? As soon as the question formed in her mind, Mathew materialized beside her. Relief made her tense muscles relax, but only a little.

Movement from Samoan caught her full attention. The demoness raised her hand and tugged at a black cord around her neck. Once the stone was out from behind Samoan's shirt, she yanked the cord free from her neck. Instantly, demons and Dark Divine appeared. There must have been several dozen—outnumbering the Divinities.

"Lex, I have a bad feeling." Desiree fell into a defensive stance, waiting.

The wind whirled around them, stirring up the leaves. Black-and-blue-colored energy flowed from the stone Samoan held over her head.

"She's calling a storm," Lex yelled.

Zach grabbed Lydia's hand and added, "It's now or never."

Combining their powers, Zach and Lydia shot a stream of bright white power straight at Samoan. The demon bitch screamed and fell to her knees. Beside Desiree, Mathew charged at the demoness.

"Matty!" Desiree shouted, but it was no use. Her son was already at Samoan's side, his hand on her shoulder.

Samoan's soul separated from her body, and once it was a few feet above her, Mathew blasted it, killing the demoness.

The stone she'd held disappeared as if called away. Fuck. *"The stone. It must have been spelled to return to Kahn."*

Lex acknowledged the telepathic thought with a grunt. She didn't have time to glance his way because a wall of demons rushed forward. She conjured a sword and fought with everything she had.

Suddenly, the ground shook, throwing everyone off balance. The Dark Divine all froze as if commanded to do so. The demons seemed confused, even though many of them continued to fight.

Desiree called to the spirits of each demon and sent them one lethal demand. A moment later, they all dropped, death by their own hands.

A cyclone of dark gray smoke swirled in the

center of the yard. When the smoke cleared, Kahn stood there, chest rising and falling as he fumed in his rage. Samoan was his mate. And they'd killed her.

The demon lord held up the Dark Sinew, then let out a scream of pain and rage. Dark magic blasted out from around him, sending a wave of lethal power out across the yard. Desiree screamed as the bolt touched Lex. Their bond snapped, severing their connection. Tears streamed down her face.

Then Mathew yelled her name, flashed in front of her, and wrapped his arms around her. A moment later, she was standing outside the Maxville Coven gatehouse.

She stared at Mathew. "What happened?"

"I couldn't save them all." Tears rolled down his cheeks, and she hugged him close. Everyone was gone. The Divinities were dead.

A pull of magic had her whirling around to come face-to face with Noah. The tears in his eyes told her that he already knew. He took her hands. "You have to go back. Kill Kahn before he is able to break through the barrier."

Desiree nodded. "Plan B."

Her heart was breaking. *Lex*. Oh, gods. "We'll fix it, bring them back."

Noah pressed a kiss to her forehead. "I have faith that you will."

Mathew took her hand, linking their fingers together. She glanced at him. "Do you know where to go?"

He nodded. "Yes, but we will only have minutes to kill him. Once Samoan dies, he will feel it."

Yes, Desiree knew that firsthand. The moment Lex died, it had felt like her soul was being ripped in two. Her chest ached. She'd just found him. They were supposed to have a lifetime together. Determination fueled the fury brewing deep within.

Meeting her son's stare, she said, "Then we have to make sure to kill him at the as soon as that bitch dies."

He took her hand and nodded. "Let's do it."

So young, yet so old. Her heart broke again for the son she'd handed over to Samoan. He'd seen too much, knew too much for a ten-year-old.

Noah touched her shoulder, drawing her attention. "Changing a decision you made years ago won't stop the war. Choices are made that take us on difficult paths, but in the end, we all end up where we need to be."

Warmth bloomed in her heart. That was something her mother would say. Not those exact words, but the meaning would be the same. "Thank you for the reminder. We'll end it now, and our loved ones will be safe."

Taking a deep breath, she nodded to Mathew. The hum of his power vibrated from his hand to hers. Then it stopped. He glanced behind them just as Teddy-Bear appeared in a flash of soft white light.

The hounds smiled, and at the same time said, "Oh, good, we're not too late. Hecate said you'd need some help. The Sinew will give us the boost we need to find and end Kahn."

Around their necks hung the quarter-sized crystal sphere. Ribbons of multi-colored magic threads swirled inside it. The Sinew seemed to glow more than it had the last time Desiree had seen it.

Mathew waved his free hand in front of them. Shimmering to life, a portal appeared. "Here we go."

Desiree was ready, even though she hadn't a clue how they would kill Khan. *I guess we'll make it up as we go along.*

CHAPTER ELEVEN

*C*oming out on the other side of the portal, Desiree scanned their surroundings. The Underworld appeared quiet and on lockdown, meaning the portals were closed. They were back in time. "How far back did we go?"

"A few seconds after Samoan dies, it'll take a bit for the energy to reach Kahn down here." Mathew raced ahead toward the large, dark castle looming over the Underworld landscape. It was a lot larger than the one she and the others had rescued Teddy-Bear from. The one that had blown up.

"So Khan has two castles?"

"The one he held the hounds in was his home until Samoan wanted a bigger one, away from the center of demonland." Mathew glanced at Desiree from over his shoulder. A smirk lifted one side of his mouth. "Khan is here. I can sense him."

Great. It was time the demon lord faced his destiny. "Then let's do this."

The hounds shook, and a blast of soft white and blue light expanded around them, leaving two huge hellhounds. They growled, and Teddy said, "Bear and I will distract the *Regal* guards while you two get inside."

Desiree nodded and followed Mathew through a side entrance. It didn't take them long to find Khan. He was in the throne room with his back to them. "I've been waiting for you two."

Shit. Cold dread froze her soul and placed a death grip on her heart. He'd known they were coming to kill him. Which meant he was ready, and most likely planned to kill them first.

Not if Desiree had anything to say about it.

He'd taken her mate. She wanted him back!

She charged at the demon, catching him off guard. Khan recovered from his surprise quickly and grabbed her by the throat, lifting her off the ground. Kicking her feet, she grabbed his wrist. "You'll never stop them from killing Samoan."

Khan's eyes turned pitch-black, and his nostrils

flared. Ah, he didn't know that little bit of info from the future yet. *Interesting*. That meant he'd lied about knowing that they were coming.

Desiree opened her *Porter* gift and allowed it to flow through her hands. The power wrapped around Khan's arm and moved to his shoulder then chest until it reached the center of his breastbone. A darker version of her power traveled up the demon's legs and met hers.

Khan roared. His grip on her slipped, and she was able to grab his hand before falling to the ground. She needed to touch him to strip his soul. Apparently, Mathew didn't.

"We can't kill him until the Dark Sinew appears." They needed the stone so no one else could use it against them.

Mathew gave a short nod while fixing his gaze on Khan.

Just then, Teddy and Bear plowed into the throne room, the double doors flying off their hinges and making the entrance wider. Stone crumbled and rolled to the middle of the room. Bear spoke first. "We need to move. Demons are going insane out there."

Without glanced back at them out of risk losing

focus on Khan, Desiree asked, "Can't you hold them off?"

Teddy shook his large head. "Not much longer."

Through the connection she had with Khan's soul, she felt the moment he became aware that Samoan was dead. Much like her link to Lex had cut off, so did Khan's to Samoan. The demon lord roared his pain and loss. However, the instant he called on his power to blast out of the Underworld, Mathew jerked his soul from his body and blew it up.

A black, dust-like cloud hung in the air for a brief moment before falling to the ground. Khan's body dissolved into the stone floor of the castle's throne room. In its place was the Dark Sinew. Desiree picked it up and slid it into her pocket.

Mathew stumbled to her. She caught him and fell to her knees, hugging him close. His power was depleted. She glanced to the hounds, who had merged together once more and shrunk to the size of a large Rottweiler with two heads.

As one, they said, "Let's go home."

She was about to ask how, but a portal opened. Glancing at the hounds, she noticed that the Sinew glowed brighter than before. They'd used the power within the stone to open a gate back home. *Thank you, goddess.*

Relief, joy, and a dark power that only a Death Demon possessed rushed through her as she stepped through the portal and into the front yard of the Divinity House. Her gaze met Lex's, and she wanted to cry in joy.

Lex glanced to Mathew and frowned. He was there in a flash, taking Matt from her arms. "What happened?"

"He used up a lot of power killing Khan."

Her mate snapped his gaze back to hers. "What? How? And where the hell were you guys? One moment you were here, and the next, you weren't."

"I'll explain inside." She leaned against Lex, her own exhaustion seeping into her.

Zach, Lydia, Khloe, and Jagger moved closer to them. Khloe motioned to the house. "You can put him in the spare room next to Lydia's. I'll set up the video feed."

She jogged up the steps.

Desiree and the others followed. Once inside, Desiree sat on the sofa and the hounds curled up on the floor at her feet. Lydia moved to the stairs. "I'm going to check on Mathew."

Even though Desiree could sense that her son

wasn't hurt physically, she was grateful for the healer's concern. "Thank you."

A few minutes later, everyone assembled around the TV where they were video-conferencing with Noah and a red-eyed Kalissa clinging to Ayden, a tissue in one hand. Before they'd started the feed, Desiree told them what had happened.

They had died.

Desiree shuddered, unable to shake the sadness the vision of all of her new friends and family falling at the hands of Kahn and his demons had caused.

Ayden had teleported to be with his pregnant mate right after hearing the news. Most likely, he had felt her distress, or at least realized that Kalissa believed he and her sister were dead.

Oh, man, what a fucking mess.

Reaching inside her jeans pocket, Desiree pulled out the Dark Sinew. "What do we do with this?"

Before Noah could answer, Hecate materialized in the center of the living room. Teddy-Bear stood at attention, their heads held high. The goddess held out her hand. "I'll take it."

Desiree handed the stone to her. Instead of taking it right away, Hecate cupped Desiree's hand. "What you and your son did for the Divinities can never be repaid. I thank you for your part in ending this war."

The inside of Desiree's wrist burned, but she forced herself not to jerk her arm away. She knew what was happening even before the link to the other Divinities formed. Hecate had inducted her into her small army of kick-ass demi-gods.

"This war may be over, but I'll still need you all to protect *magickin* and humans. And to keep the Earthside demons in line." Hecate took the dark stone and faced Teddy-Bear.

Taking the Sinew in one hand, she placed the dark one in the same palm, the two stones touching. She closed her fist around them and squeezed. After she'd muttered a few words in Latin, multi-colored light shone from between her fingers. Then it stopped.

When Hecate opened her hand, there was one larger stone in her palm. She slipped it from around the hounds' necks and placed it around her own. "I guess you two would like to stay?"

They nodded and said at the same time, "Yes, Mom. They kind of grew on us."

Hecate laughed. "Very well." She faced the TV and talked to Noah. "The Dark Divine are no longer controlled by the Sinew, dark or otherwise. They are, however, under my protection, as is all *magickin*. They no longer need to keep hidden."

Noah offered a warm smile. "I will pass on the word."

Scanning the room, Hecate smiled. "Take care, my children." Then she dematerialized.

Desiree sank into the sofa. Her eyes drifted shut a moment before a warm hand cupped her cheek. Opening her lids, she met Lex's stare. He raised his brows and said, "Let's get Mathew and go home."

"Where is home?"

"Your home in the Oceanway Coven."

Love filled her heart.

No more running.

No more lies.

She was going home. With her son and mate.

Framing Lex's face in her hands, she kissed him, allowing her lips to linger on his longer than she'd intended. She pulled back to stare into his chocolate gaze with its rivers of red. "I love you."

Instantly, he lifted her off the couch and crushed his mouth to hers. "I love you, too."

"Let's go home."

Continue reading for an excerpt from my action packed urban fantasy series starter, Rise of the Shade, A Randi Sanderson novel.

Get updates on releases via Lia's newsletter
http://bit.ly/LiaDavisNewsletter

ABOUT RISE OF THE SHADE

Murder is a game that Randi Sanderson knows far too well, but at least she's playing on the right side of the law. Being half-archangel and half-vampire makes her one of Jacksonville Sheriff Office's best detectives and a suspect's worst nightmare.

When she arrives at the scene of her next case, it's obvious this murder isn't a typical human crime of passion or rage. As a powerful hybrid, Randi can sense something is off, and not just because the body was dumped in a church parking lot. Luckily, her many gifts include the ability to dig up dirt on anyone.

This time, getting to work won't be so simple. Surprised by a new partner, Randi knows her life is about to get a little more complicated. There's a reason she doesn't work with others. To the outside world, she's just a police detective and single mom, but the reality is she has a secret identity to keep.

With the case taking a dark turn and her new partner obviously keeping secrets of his own, the last thing Randi needs is more trouble. So when the angelic and demonic factions start bidding to hire her to kill other supernatural beings just like herself, she patently refuses. The rogue hybrids known as The Shade are none of her concern, and she isn't interested in becoming an assassin.

But when she finds herself in the middle of her own case with The Shade coming for her, she must reconsider. The half-angel, half-demon miscreants won't stop until they're dead or they have what they truly want: Randi's son.

CHAPTER 1

The steeple of the church rose into a pitch-black sky, adorned with a tiny, white cross dimly illuminated by the floodlights below. I always thought steeples resembled middle fingers, an angsty 'eff you' to the heavens, but I was, apparently, alone in that comparison. Humans loved building them; angels loved looking at them like proud parents. As an angel/vampire hybrid, I—quite reasonably—had mixed feelings regarding churches, steeple or no. But I set those musings aside as I lowered my gaze along the façade of the little, white structure to the parking lot in front of it.

Jacksonville's finest crawled over the area like ants, busy with their individual tasks. Uniformed officers lined the perimeter, their cop cars spinning reds and blues. Blue-jacketed forensic specialists carefully scoured the pavement and body for clues. The giant floods towered overhead, blasting enough light to rival the sun. They formed a broad circle, banishing the night from our crime scene. Yet at the center of all this was a terrible darkness, a hideousness that brought me here.

A girl. A dead girl. A pretty, dead girl with sharp, blue eyes and dark-brown hair that dangled curls around her pale features. Her body sprawled out in the middle of our scene, arms and legs splayed haphazardly on the pavement. Her gaze directed into the night sky, wide eyes lifeless and fearful, a snapshot of her last moment. I lifted the police tape, nodding toward the officer standing there, then crossed the circle of light to the poor woman's corpse.

"Hold up," I told the forensics team, buzzing around her. They paused, turned to look at me, then looked at one another with a certain degree of confusion. Then I knelt beside her and placed my hand over her eyes, closing them with a sweep of my palm. I love forensics specialists; they make my life so much easier. That said, they could be a bunch of emotionally-stunted science geeks with little appreciation for such delicate matters.

I rose back up and stepped aside, allowing them to continue their work. No blood. No visible wounds. No immediate signs of struggle of any kind. With her eyes now shut, she might as well have been sleeping. Except her heart wasn't beating, she wasn't drawing breath, and all thought had vacated her brain.

"Detective." I spun around to see who addressed me. A short, stout man clad in street blues rested one hand on his nightstick while the other pinched the brim of his hat. I stifled a laugh at his propriety. Nobody wore the hat. There were a thousand cop hats collecting dust in lockers back at their respective stations. But he was being respectful, I had to give him that.

With focus, I peered into his thoughts and saw that he cared a great deal about his job. On that point, we were simpatico. Then, blaring loudly at the forefront of his thoughts was a less admirable imagining of yours truly, sans suit. I bristled, but a part of me enjoyed a little flattery. It was nice to know I still had it after thirty-eight years on this Earth, winding through a bizarre life path that included a whirlwind romance, untimely death, heavy depression in its wake, but also the most precious thing of all—my son, Logan. He was always hanging around my thoughts, sticking close to my heart.

But I digress.

"You're the responding officer?" I asked the cute, little lech.

He nodded dutifully. "Officer Mike Daniels."

Mike extended his hand. I shook it. "Detective Randi Sanderson. Pleasure." With touch, my telepathy strengthened, and I could feel Mike doing his best to suppress his attraction in favor of his job. *Aw, sweet boy.* "Who put in the call?"

A stiff arm raised toward the church. Before the tall entrance, joined by another pair of officers, stood a priest. "Father O'Brien," said Officer Daniels.

A morose scowl etched dark lines through the old man's features, made all the more grim by his all black get-up. What were those called? With the wavy, black robes and the white collar? I sifted through my thoughts for the answer, thinking my mother would know. Angels knew all the terminology, iconography, and mythology—true, tainted, or outright false. I never really took an interest. I suppose my vampire side was a bit roguish. The priest stared over at me, tilting his chin ever so slightly. They all tried to look so goddamn wise, exuding a certain owlish solemnity that their flock so respected. *How little you know*, I thought, staring back. A whole world of inhuman creatures surrounded him, visiting from above and below, all manner of angels and demons that he wouldn't recognize if they punched him in his face. Not that I planned to. I kept the inner vampire in check.

"What was Father O'Brien up to so late at the church?" I asked, holding the priest's gaze.

"Said he likes walking the courtyard at night sometimes. Clears his head."

Clear head, guilty conscience? The consideration left as quickly as it occurred, dismissed as I sensed his profound, if a bit performative, dismay at the night's turn. "Alright," I said with a sigh, "keep him around for just a bit longer, I'll make my way over in a minute."

Officer Daniels nodded then shuffled across the parking lot to the front door to speak with the priest. Left alone again, I stretched my back, twisting and sighing, secretly reaching out with my angelic senses to suss out any details. Emotional imprints linger for days after their initial expression. The stronger the emotion, the more potent the imprint.

I turned my feet and began marching around the perimeter of the light, eyes wandering over the scene, invisible tendrils of angelic essence extending from my person. They swept like a hundred whiskers picking up any signals from the ethereal plane. My brow furrowed to the results. *Nothing?* Whatever traces lingered were too minimal for my abilities. That could only mean one thing. The murder hadn't taken place at this location. The deceased was transported to this parking lot. How theatrical, dumping a body in a church parking lot. I was surprised there weren't eccentricities to behold, some grotesque manipulation to the crime scene only a sick-minded pervert would concoct. The type of thing true crime junkies lived for, the weird, the wild, the *nasty*. While I loved my job as a homicide detective, the lurid wasn't what drew me. It was the puzzle. Fitting together the pieces, solving the riddle, with the bonus of putting behind bars people that couldn't be trusted to live among us.

I suppose that's rich for a half-vampire to say. Generally speaking, however, expatriates of both Heaven and Hell maintained relatively discrete lives on the middle, as they often call it.

Having utilized my angelic abilities, I turned away from the light and peered into the darkness, flipping over to my vampiric senses. Demon sight provided a better view of the night. Any murderers lurking around the scene of the crime would stalk the darkness under the assumption they were essentially invisible. There were parts of living as a human with a secret divine/profane ancestry that were difficult but being underestimated was a nice silver lining.

In the middle of downtown Jax, a handful of homeless shuffled past alleys, but among them was nobody of note. With a flared nostril, I drew in a whiff of the air, uncertain what I might be sniffing for, but it seemed prudent all the same. Vampiric olfactory experienced the familiar potpourri of a hot, Florida night in the city. Exhaust, litter, faint traces of the sea, and the St. John's River. No strange beasts, no stench of fear nor lust. Nothing to give away a hidden culprit watching over the investigation of their handiwork.

Turning back to the busy center of the parking lot, I took a breath. *So, I'll have to employ good old-fashioned police work on this one*, I thought. My supernatural toolbox provided a usual edge from the onset of an investigation, but this time I'd need to employ a little brain power. That was alright with me. In fact, more than alright. I enjoyed proving myself without the handicap of heavenly and hellish crutches. After all, as a hybrid, I didn't really belong to either community. I might as well have been human.

"Any ID?" I inquired, approaching one of the blue-coats knelt beside the body. She was swabbing a stain on the pavement beneath and beside the vic's right armpit. Probably an oil leak, I surmised, but 'no stone unturned' and all.

The forensic tech had black hair in a tight pony, stern features, and an unshakable laser focus. Which is why she didn't redirect her attention until I cleared my throat and leaned forward into her periphery. She twisted her head upward to meet my gaze. "Oh, sorry, detective."

"That's alright. Is there any ID, though?" Sometimes, you have to repeat yourself around these people. I'm a generally impatient, no-nonsense person, but I bent for them, my worker bees, the real magic makers in the crime fighting world.

She turned back to the body, turning her head to view the inside of a jean-jacket pocket. Carefully, she reached in with a latex-gloved hand and removed a shiny, purple wallet. Reverently, she unclasped and unfolded it. Her fingers ran along the cards tucked into position, arriving at a driver's license. She pinched it between index and thumb, gave a tug, and freed it from the wallet. Then she stood and held the card before me.

"Catherine Jacobs," I read aloud. "D.O.B. December 18, 1985. Our vic was…" I ran a quick calculation in my head, "thirty-five."

"And a Sagittarius."

I turned to the tech with a raised left eyebrow. "Not very scientific of you."

She shrugged. "We all have our thing."

I thought of my *thing*. Compared to hers, it was a whopper. I couldn't fault her for astrological leanings when my mother literally came from the heavens. Despite that inside track, I couldn't say for certain whether star charts and all that rang false. The world was bigger than I knew, too.

I directed the tech to pass off the ID to a uni to run through the database, then as she clasped the wallet again another tech was already by her side opening a baggie to place the evidence into. *Like a machine, these people*.

"Detective Sanderson?" The voice was masculine, deep, but tinged with youth. Direct, but gallant. My eyes narrowed even before I turned to face him, knowing exactly who he'd be. Another detective, sent to partner with me. The character was unmistakable, instantly readable.

Sure enough, I pivoted to find a tall, well-postured man with near-white blonde hair cut short, a square jaw, and dark eyes that looked like deep pits. Unnervingly deep pits. Alluringly deep pits.

Wait. Scratch that last one.

"I'm Detective Bennett," he introduced himself. "Cash Bennett." As we shook hands, his strong grip encasing mine, he added, "Your new partner."

I nodded. "Uh huh."

Cash smiled, forming a dimple in his right cheek. "It's a pleasure to meet you."

"I'll bet."

He chuckled mirthfully. Not the reaction I anticipated. "Technically, my first day is supposed to be tomorrow, but the chief called to suggest I come down here tonight to meet you. He thought you could use the help on this case."

I scrutinized his eyes with my own, trying to read past them. With our hands still clasped, I attempted to enter his thoughts, perusing hidden motives. Perhaps it was the exhaustion of the hour in concert with the previous use of telepathy, but I hit a wall. A twinge of pain throbbed at my temple, and I winced, releasing his hand, and pressing my fingers to my forehead.

"What's wrong?" he asked.

I waved away his concern with my free hand. "Just a little headache, it'll go away in a minute."

"Here." He wrapped one hand around the back of my neck while the other pressed against my temples and both massaged. Tension immediately drained from the muscles in my neck and the headache receded. I sighed with relief until our eyes met again and I glared back.

Cash retracted his hands and stepped back, hanging his head. "Sorry, old habits."

I squinted one eye. "Old habits?"

He scratched the back of his head, bending his toned, muscular arm to do so. I refused to look. "I worked briefly as a massage therapist before entering the force."

I crossed my arms. "Interesting pivot."

"Yeah, well, I—"

"That was the conversation closer, not an opener, young buck," I said, tapping his shoulder while passing him. I came to stand above the victim, staring down at her soft face. "At this moment, I'm not so much interested in your life story as I am Catherine Jacobs's death story."

Cash stepped up beside me. "Young buck?" he repeated. "I'll wager I'm older than you."

"How old are you?" I asked, turning to face him.

He peered down from his six-plus feet of height. "Forty."

"Only two years, hot shot. And in terms of experience, you're still the young buck around here, capisce?"

Cash only grinned back.

I sighed. "Chief sent you down here tonight, huh?"

Cash nodded. "Yup."

I shook my head, turning away from him. "Mark, you cheeky sonova—"

"Said you've got a lot of experience. Said I could learn a lot from you."

I smirked, turning back to Cash. "A little flattery to help swallow the pill, hmm?"

Cash shrugged. "You and Chief Dobbs go back?"

"To diapers," I told him. "He seems to think I'm still wearing them."

I pulled out my phone and shot off a quick text to Mark: **You think you're funny, don't you?**

Before I could pocket the phone again, his reply popped up on screen: **Detective Bennett is good police.**

I glared at the screen. Mark was lucky not to be in my presence. **Good or not, you know why I can't be partnered, Mark**

There was a moment's break in the conversation, a silent recognition of the fact. Mark knew all about me, knew my parents, knew the secret we kept. He was human, but a trusted one. A few allies in positions of power helped keep everything on an even keel. Three dots popped up while he typed his brief reply: **Play nice.**

I grumbled, stabbing my thumbs against the keyboard: **We'll chat about this BS later, friend**.

The phone dropped back into my pocket and the frustrations were stuffed into the closet for the time being, making way for the case. Poor Catherine Jacobs. My face slumped, peering into hers. Perhaps if I waited, some vestiges of her last moments would radiate from her, setting off my angelic sense.

"What can I do to help you?" Cash inquired.

"Talk up the priest," I said without averting my gaze from Catherine. "He's over by the church entrance, he called this in. Get a statement, ask if he's seen anyone lurking around the church recently, see if—well, you're a detective, I won't tell you how to detect."

"Aye, aye," he said, heading off for the priest.

Soon as he left my side, a cop replaced him. "Clean record, detective," he said. "Married, no kids."

"Husband?"

"What else?"

I turned to the cop, a doofy-looking expression on his face. "It is 2021, officer."

He tried covering his embarrassment with a cough and a hung head. "Fella by the name of Eric Jacobs. Lives over in Empire Point."

I looked across the lot to Cash, speaking with the priest. He peered over Father O'Brien's head to return my gaze. "Looks like we've got a next stop, partner," I said to myself.

Want more? Get your copy of Rise fo the Shade Here: https://authorliadavis.com/bookshelf/the-randi-sanderson-series/

ABOUT LIA DAVIS

USA Today bestselling author Lia Davis spends most of her time writing racy romance and witty women's fiction, the majority of which takes place in fantasy worlds full of magic and mayhem. She prides herself on her ability to craft strong and sassy heroines, emotionally intelligent alpha heroes, and rich, expansive universes that readers want to visit again and again.

She is the mastermind behind the bestselling Ashwood Falls Series and the co-author of the beloved Witching After Forty Series.

She currently resides in Florida where she's working on her very own happily-ever-after with her supportive husband and spends her free time doting on a pack of feisty felines and her loving family.

Find all of Lia's online hangouts here:
https://solo.to/authorliadavis
Check out the official Davis Raynes Merch Etsy Store:
https://www.etsy.com/shop/davisraynesmerch

ALSO BY LIA DAVIS

Paranormal Women's Fiction

Witching After Forty (Co-written with L.A. Boruff)

Fanged After Forty (Co-written with L.A. Boruff)

Shifting Through Midlife (Co-written with L.A. Boruff and Lacey Carter)

Packless in Seattle

Paranormal Romance Series

Shifters of Ashwood Falls

Bears of Blackrock

Dragons of Ares

Gods and Dragons

Dark Scales Division (Co-written with Kerry Adrienne)

Shifting Magick Trilogy

The Divinities

Witches of Rose Lake

Coven's End (Co-written with L.A. Boruff)

Academy's Rise (Co-written with L.A. Boruff)

Wolf Ranch

Singles Titles

First Contact (MM co-written with Kerry Adrienne)

Ghost in the Bottle (co-written with Kerry Adrienne)

Dragon's Web

Royal Enchantment

Marked by Darkness

His Big Bad Wolf (MM)

Their Royal Ash

Tempting the Wolf

Hexed with Sass (part of the Milly Taiden Sassy Ever After World)

Claiming Her Dragons (Part of the Milly Taiden Paranormal Dating Agency)

Rogue Alliance (Part of the Wolves of Chaos Valley Shared World)

Rune of Passing (Part of the Immortal Keepers Shared World)

Contemporaries

Pleasures of the Heart Series

Single Titles

His Guarded Heart (MM)